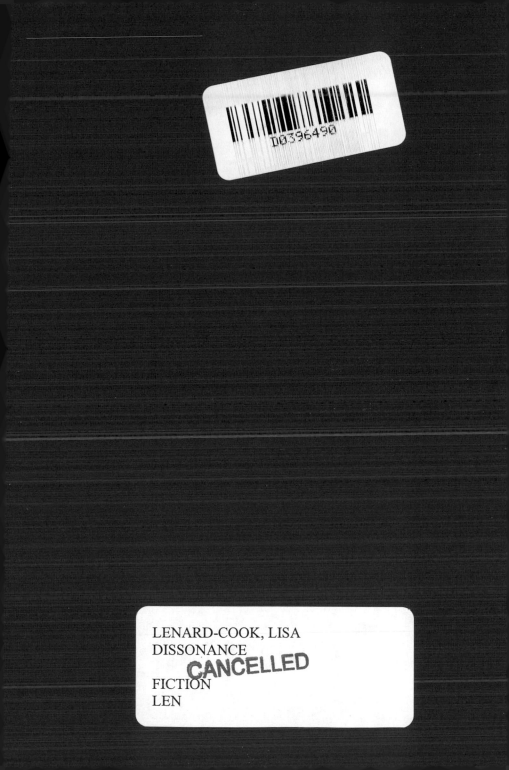

Dissonance

Dissonance

a novel

LISA LENARD-COOK

Winner of the Jim Sagel Prize for the Novel, 2001

UNIVERSITY OF NEW MEXICO PRESS | ALBUQUERQUE

Library of Congress
Cataloging-in-Publication Data

Lenard-Cook, Lisa.
Dissonance : a novel / by Lisa Lenard-Cook.
— 1st ed.
   p. cm.
ISBN 0-8263-3090-8 (cloth : alk. paper)
1. Women—New Mexico—Fiction.
2. Theresienstadt (Concentration camp)—Fiction.
3. Holocaust, Jewish (1939-1945)—Fiction.
4. Inheritance and succession—Fiction.
5. Prague (Czech Republic)—Fiction.
6. Women music teachers—Fiction.
7. Women composers—Fiction.
8. Santa Fe (N.M.)—Fiction.
9. Jewish women—Fiction. I. Title.

PS3612.E359 D57 2003

813'.6—dc21

2003005841

The excerpt from Mark Doty's "Lament-
Heaven" appears in *My Alexandria*
(University of Illinois, 1993).
Used by permission.

Excerpts of this novel have
appeared in *Puerto del Sol* and
www.thescreamonline.com

Printed by Sheridan Printers, Inc.

Set in Janson 11/14.5
Display type set in Cezanne
and Futura Condensed

Design and composition: Robyn Mundy

2   3   4   5   6   7   8   9

. . . I can't remember
even the melody, which doesn't matter;
there's nothing to hold
but the memory of the sensation

of such moments, canceling out
the whine of the self
that doesn't want to be ground down,

answering the little human cry
at the heart of the elegy,
Oh why aren't I what I wanted to be,

exempt from history?

MARK DOTY

Dissonance

THE piano is unique among instruments *one*
for its double stroke. The player touches
a key, *C*, let us say, and the key's depression moves a hammer
onto a string: *Do*, says the piano. Or, the player may strike a
number of keys simultaneously: *C*, *E*, *G*, and then the piano
will sound a C-major chord.

In the 20th century, composers have moved to more dissonant chord constructions. The listener balks. But it is, in its
way, a fitting metaphor for what this century has wrought.

My name is Anna Kramer, and I am a piano teacher. Monday
through Friday afternoons, from three-thirty until six, I
entertain children in various stages of their movement toward
adulthood with the mysteries of the instrument. My Steinway
Grand sits in a plant-filled room with good, filtered southern
light, and in winter as the shadows lengthen, the plants etch
mottled patterns across both the keys and the faces of the

young students. The keys are white and black; the students are white—Anglo, as we call them here—and the shadows are a translucent grey that border on an illusion. When the shadows surrender to the dark, I turn on the single focused light above the music stand, its glare causing momentary blinking in the student. "Again," I say, as if I have not noticed the darkness, as if I have not noticed the way a sudden spotlight can startle a living creature into stillness.

"Again," I say, and the student's eyes move to the top of the sheet of music, to the opening refrain of *Für Elise* or the *Moonlight Sonata*. I am traditional in the music I choose for my young students. The dissonance will come soon enough, with or without me.

My husband is a nuclear physicist, as was my father, though my husband is Jewish, which my father was not. My father, Leon Holtz, was a Major General in the United States Army, and, during World War II, he was in charge of what went on here in Los Alamos. My father was among the men who pored over a map of Japan and decided: *Hiroshima, Nagasaki.* My father was proud of his work and the way he performed it. My father was proud that his decisions helped end a war that had already gone on far too long. Is it only I who now wonders at his ease, at the facility with which he touched that map and said, "There. And there"? Is it only I who sees her own existence as a counterpoint to those other lives? *Survivor's guilt,* I have heard this called, though I have not suffered as those true survivors do. No. I am only the progeny of the man who made certain few of them did survive.

We have no children, my husband and I. When I was a girl, there were air-raid drills, and we sat cross-legged under our desks with our heads down, hands knitted behind our necks. I did not think that I would see adulthood, when I was a girl, and so I did not consider children a possibility.

Of course, it is possible that my sterility is a result of growing up here in Los Alamos, but nobody knows for certain. But my husband and I do not have children. The closest I can come is my students, who, of course, are not really mine at all.

My husband's name is Paul Kramer. His parents, of whom only his mother is still alive, were in Auschwitz together, though they somehow did not know each other at the time. After Auschwitz, both emigrated to Buffalo, New York, where my mother-in-law, Rose, had a second cousin, and my father-in-law, Isaac, an old friend from the town where he had been raised. Buffalo is where Paul grew up, and I met him at a party in Ithaca years later. I was his roommate's date.

The mailman rang the doorbell; the letter was registered, return receipt, and he needed a signature. It was from a law firm in Albuquerque, and something about it kept me from opening it right away. I made a cup of tea, and when it was ready, I took it and the letter to the kitchen table and sat down.

I slit the envelope carefully with a knife; it seemed to demand it. Inside was a Notice to the Heirs of Hana

Weissova. The name set off an odd humming, distant, but no recognition. I read on.

To the pianist Anna Holtz Kramer, of Los Alamos, New Mexico, I do give, devise, and bequeath my journals and my original music scores, to use as she shall see fit.

I skimmed the rest of the gives, devises, and bequeaths, but that was all. I read the other names: a sister, Raja Weissova BenTov, in Haifa, Israel; a godson, David Stone, in Albuquerque. Hana Weissova. I heard the humming again, an aria perhaps. But I couldn't place the name.

I dialed the number on the letterhead and asked for the lawyer who had signed the letter. I agreed to drive down to Albuquerque on Saturday, when an estate sale would be occurring at Hana Weissova's home. The lawyer gave me directions. I hung up and made another cup of tea.

The drive to Albuquerque still thrills me, though there's much more traffic now and the interstate is completed all the way from Santa Fe. The land on either side of the interstate is painted in muted pastels, and changes according to the time of day. Distances are different, infinite even, and the emptiness is at once startling and soothing.

Midway between Santa Fe and Albuquerque, an outlet mall sprawls where there used to be a stuccoed bar sheltered by cottonwoods, the latter the place we always stopped when I was a girl, for Cokes and to pee or to just stretch our legs. The building's still there, boarded up, and I worry, absurdly, that one day when I drive to Albuquerque it will be gone.

Do buildings leave some essence behind when they are no longer there? Certainly people do. My father speaks to me every day, his voice unchanged, still directing my life from his command post. My mother appears in gestures of my own: hair brushed off a cheek; legs crossed twice, at both the ankle and the knee; or a certain bend to the fingers as they come down on the Steinway's keys, a touch that the piano translates to music, and for which the child yearns.

The boarded-up bar was still there; I drove by about 10:30 that morning and traffic exiting for the outlet mall backed up in the right lanes on both sides of the interstate. To the southeast, clouds curled over the top of the Sandias, and to the west, the sky over the Jemez was a dull and uniform grey. The air smelled of cold and snow, and I closed my vent, something I do not like to do. I tuned the radio to KUNM; they were playing Sousa marches, which I ordinarily avoid but which somehow seemed appropriate to the weather. A half-hour later, I exited the interstate at San Mateo and went into a coffee bar in a strip mall to clear the freeway buzz—and perhaps the Sousa—from my head.

While I drank a cup of hot tea, I read the letter again. I unfolded my Albuquerque map, which I'd brought in from the car, and looked up each of the street names. Albuquerque, except for its very old center, is a planned city, easy to navigate once you've memorized the main roads, set at one-mile intervals from the western volcanoes to the eastern mountains and from the Air Force base in the south to Sandia Pueblo in the north.

The estate sale was in the South Valley, where the majority of horror stories on the nightly news take place (all New Mexico television stations are based in Albuquerque, its largest city), and, except for a visit to the zoo as a teen, I was certain I'd never been there.

I studied the map, looking for a route that might be relatively free of drive-by shootings, trying to recall which streets were most often mentioned by the newscasters. I looked up and around at the others in the coffee bar. A man in jogging clothes sat at the next table, reading the Albuquerque *Journal*, while on my other side another man, in jeans and leather jacket, stared unseeing out the window, drumming his fingers on the table. I opted for the jogging suit.

"I've never been there," he admitted when I asked, but stood to study the map over my shoulder. "I'm sure this would be okay," he went on, pointing to Bridge and then to Atrisco. "What's the name of the street again?"

I showed him where it was on the map. "It dead-ends at an *acequia*," he said, indicating the blue of the irrigation ditch, "so you can only get to it from Atrisco. You get off at the César Chávez exit, and go right. You'll be fine, but you might want to keep your doors locked."

It turned out to not be so bad at all. Immediately off the freeway the houses were shabby and small, with faded paint barely covering their stucco, nothing but dirt and dried clots of soon-to-be tumbleweeds in the small, chain-link-fenced yards, and iron bars on every window and door. Then, suddenly, everything changed. The road bustled with businesses, produce stands, *taquerias*, used clothing stores. Hand-painted signs leaned against pickups, offering *piñon* nuts and firewood displayed on lowered tailgates. Beyond the business area, which was perhaps a half mile long, the road crossed the bridge. Now, open places appeared and the cross-streets that went north and south disappeared into cottonwoods. Atrisco was the third of these, and I turned right, then found the street I was seeking and turned left.

When I saw the house, I was immediately glad I had come. A high adobe wall abutted the uncurbed road and surrounded the front courtyard. High cottonwoods, their leaves brown and rattling in the wind, arced over the top, and a faded wood *entrada* stood open, the ornate estate sale sign's arrow pointing invitingly inside.

I found a parking place where the road dead-ended at the *acequia* and walked the half-block back to the house. The weather was such that you know you will remember it forever after as the distinct feel of a certain type of November Saturday morning, the wind both a threat and a promise, and the air unusually damp, chilling even the bones.

But inside the wall, everything changed. The agents had set the outdoor items for sale in neat rows—Adirondack chairs and huge terra cotta planters with browned stalks withered in their dirt, chile *ristras* of all sizes hung on metal coatracks, and garden implements leaned tidily against black wrought-iron tables.

The brick path led to an open front door, which was painted a lovely sky blue—*azul*, the Spanish word, fits this blue so much better—and I followed it in. Both the merely curious and the more serious sale aficionados milled inside, moving from room to room, inspecting furniture and the smaller items set out on tables. Discrete agents offered help without being pushy, and I asked one, a young woman with a blonde buzz cut and flowing flowered skirt, about an abalone dresser set that reminded me of one my mother had once had. I decided I did not need it, at the price. The house was somehow familiar, in that way strange houses sometimes are. It was almost as if I had been there before, in a dream perhaps, though I am not, like so many in New Mexico are, one who puts much stock in such things.

The piano was in a conservatory at the back of the house, and the conservatory itself was both unexpected and perfectly suited. Although it followed the eastern style—large, windowed, facing out to a well-kept garden—it was southwestern as well, with thick adobe walls, *viga*-beamed ceilings, their wood dark and weathered, a *kiva* fireplace in one corner in which an inviting fire was indeed burning. The floors were a dark *Saltillo* tile, covered with worn Navajo rugs, and bookcases had been built into the walls, bookcases that now displayed neat stacks of what looked to be very old papers.

I asked the agent in that room where the lawyer was. The agent was an earnest middle-aged man, a white carnation in his lapel—he rather reminded me of Tony Randall—and he led me to a man seated discretely at a table in a far corner. I introduced myself, and he snapped open his briefcase without further conversation, then carefully lifted out a stack of plastic-encased scores. All at once I had to hold one myself, and I reached for one, nearly grabbed for it, and he seemed to jump back, though of course that is not as it was at all. He handed it to me carefully, as if it were a flower long-preserved which could quickly turn to dust. I touched the music through the plastic, and then I heard it, an arrangement unlike any I had ever heard before. The first touch of music is quite unlike any other in its echoes, in its evocation of memories not yet known.

"Did you know Hana Weissova?" the lawyer asked me. How could he have known? I did not, I said, and so he told me that she had been a composer and music teacher in Czechoslovakia before the War, not terribly well-known but making a name for herself, until she was interred at Terezín.

"Terezín?" I asked.

"Theresienstadt?" he said. "Perhaps you know that name?" I shook my head. "A minor concentration camp, as concentration camps went," he said. "Noted for its many artists, writers, and composers. The Nazi brass used to go there for concerts, can you imagine?"

I felt the music through the plastic sheet, its haunting cacophony of strings, and the piano, insisting its melody above them. "She wrote this there?" I asked.

"Oh no," the man said. "In fact, her manuscripts from before the war were destroyed. She tried to recreate them, after, but these are what came out instead. Do you play?"

I nodded.

"Perhaps you would like to play that one you're holding? To hear it?"

"I can hear it," I said, perhaps a bit too harshly.

But he only said, "I'd like to hear it, too," and pointed to a black Steinway Grand set by a potted weeping fig.

It is hard to describe what music does, though we have all felt its various demands. Some music rouses us, while another makes us remember and still another can set us unaccountably weeping. The same concerto played well or badly can either elate or disappoint, and a good blues singer can obtusely cheer us up.

Hana Weissova's sonata, that first one I saw and played on that odd November morning, yielded emotions I had done my best to bury years before. The strings, which I heard only in my head that day, bore down insistently, tried to enclose the piano, or the player, or the listener, or, perhaps, the composer, but the piano would not be confined. Glissandos ran its length, while the bass improvised chord constructions I was surprised to find my small hand could cover.

It was a brief sonata, and when I stopped there was silence in the room and then applause. I looked up, startled to find the room so full of people, startled to be in that unfamiliar room at all.

The lawyer hovered behind me. "Thank you," I whispered. "I don't know why they're mine, but thank you." Then I started the piece over and the room receded once again.

Dissonance, Stravinsky once noted, is an element of transition, a complex or interval of tones which is not complete in itself. It plays the part, Stravinsky went on, of an allusion, and is no more an agent of disorder than consonance is a guarantee of security. Even dissonance must ultimately be resolved to the ear's satisfaction. Even dissonance, in other words, yearns toward harmony.

I fill my mornings with music: After I have washed and dried the breakfast dishes and perhaps, if necessary, dusted or swept, I move to the room where my Steinway waits and select a piece from the shelves of music that are beside it.

While my ear favors Mozart and Chopin, my hands seem

most competent with more modern composers: Copland and Bernstein, Shostakovich and Fine. When I play these latter pieces, my hands become quite separate things, and I, detached, will watch them dance across the keys like mating cranes, advancing and retreating but never touching. The music that these hands make seems not to fill the room as more classical music does but rather to seek a way out. It reminds me of children, then, and of children's games, though I suspect my memory of those games is not what they really are at all. Even with the one true friend I had as a child, I did not play them.

Paul tries to be home for dinner by seven, but there are nights that he forgets. The nights that he remembers, he will tell me about his work—the things he is permitted to tell me—and I will try to understand. These days he is working on something called containment, a procedure which involves half lives that go on for many thousands of years.

Though I strive to understand the mechanics of what Paul tells me, I find myself instead caught up with its language: containment, half-lives. I try to imagine not dying, but instead having one's existence halved, again and again. What is left, at the end of that infinite halving? Or does it never end? Death seems a much more preferable conclusion, in comparison.

My father, too, often talked of his work. By the time I was born, in 1948, his project was not so secret as it had once been, though its particulars were. When my father talked of his work, at dinner, at six, it was as if it were any other job: He complained of surly employees, or told of particular small successes that had happened that day. Sometimes he related a joke he'd heard, and my mother and I would always laugh politely at its conclusion. I have sometimes wondered if he noticed that we otherwise made no sound during those meals.

My mother, were she still alive, would have been about the same age as Hana Weissova, and so I assign Hana my mother's features, which were delicate and finely etched. My mother had the pale smooth skin and dark dark hair that were hallmarks of beauty in her day, and she had lovely long fingers that leaped across the piano keys with an abandon she did not otherwise exhibit.

My mother-in-law, though also the same age, is of such a different appearance that I would not think to put her into my imagined Hana. My mother-in-law is small but sturdy—peasant stock, as she herself points out—and, much unlike my mother, she is quick to voice her opinions both loudly and definitively.

My mother-in-law is also very funny. She makes me laugh. She is the only person I have ever known who can do this, and, when I think about her life, and in particular those years in Auschwitz when death rained from the very sky, I cannot understand why this should be so.

"But it is very funny," my mother-in-law will tell me when I ask. She has a Polish accent that I find peculiarly enchanting, and she will say, with this accent, "It is all a big joke, don't you see? Why should we think it matters, or that we do? We do not—and that is the joke."

This is not one of the things she says that makes me laugh.

Hana Weissova had two children, a daughter and a son, and her husband, a man she loved for his stolid predictability, taught economics at Charles University in Prague, which was (and is) the oldest university in Europe. She herself had studied in Vienna, and the prestige of that association assured her employment, when she desired it, though in 1938, with her children so young, she preferred, for the most part, to stay home.

What Hana had bequeathed me included five sonatas, a fantasy, a set of exercises modeled on Bach but that experimented with chromatic chords, and a much annotated symphony that had apparently never been completed to her satisfaction. There were also two sets of notebooks—one set comprising her thoughts on her compositions, and the other, much larger set, a sporadically kept diary.

She'd begun the diary in August 1945, when she returned to Prague from Terezín, and its early entries were an attempt to recreate the life she'd had before she'd been relocated to the camp. Apparently she had found this exercise too painful, and, after scratching diagonal lines across her few futile attempts, she had written simply: *Anton, 1915–1944; Pavel, 1937–?; and Heidi, 1939-1944.*

Perhaps it was because I had time. I had too much time, in fact, and I found myself often thinking about Hana Weissova. At first, my imaginings were vague and momentary: I would picture her at her piano, her long ringless fingers flying across the keys.

But as I read the diary, the scenes became more vivid. While Hana's crossed-out recordings of her life in Terezín were cryptic and quick compared to her evocations of her life after the war, they nonetheless were enough to fuel my imagination. People spoke; they moved about rooms; they grew as real to me as my own family—maybe more so. Hana acquired dimensions, an essence, a core. I found myself thinking about her more and more often, and found her story recreating itself in my mind. I know that the reproduction of sound involves its translation into electrical impulses, which can then be played back as a recording of the original sound. My imagining of Hana's life, I would like to think, employed a similar principle, one in which I was the medium that facilitated the reproduction.

She was worried about Heidi's chicken pox. She knew it was foolish; she hadn't worried about Pavel's, but he seemed so much sturdier than his baby sister, and always had. She sat up through the night next to the baby's crib, listening to Bartok turned down low on the radio set, and to the occasional news reports that interrupted the music. It seemed certain that the British were going to hand Czechoslovakia to Hitler, that dreadful man. To Hana, it made no sense: Czechoslovakia was not England's to give.

When Anton woke her at dawn, she realized she must have dozed off in the chair, and realized, too, an odd dream he had interrupted: a small Rumpelstiltskin-like creature with Hitler's moustache and impenetrable eyes, stamping its foot through the floor of the nursery and demanding the child in the crib. Hana reached out to touch the sleeping baby's forehead, to brush away the remarkable blonde curls, and Anton in turn touched Hana's shoulder. "Come to bed," he said, and she did.

It was a scene she would replay in detail, over and over again, for the rest of her life.

She played, that evening, with the Symphony, a program of Beethoven and Brahms. The Tyl Theatre was filled to capacity, and the audience was spotted with stiff men in the uniform of the SS, tall blonde women in low-cut black gowns hanging eagerly to their arms. At the intermission, Hana went out to the lobby to have a cigarette with Anton, and as she approached him, standing alone by a pillar, a large group of officers and women nearby erupted into sudden raucous laughter. Anton at once reached out his arm and pulled her to him.

When they went out for drinks afterwards, the same group occupied the tables next to them, tables which had been pushed together to accommodate them. Hana and Anton sat silently at their table, their hands entwined beneath it, and listened to the sound of the German consonants which seemed to contain no vowels or softness, and the laughter which interrupted it. After one drink, Anton paid their bill and, still holding hands, they walked home in the still-warm September night. There is so much to say, Hana thought as they walked. And there are no words to say it.

When they arrived home, they went upstairs to check on the sleeping children, and Hana told Marya, the nanny, to go to bed. Heidi's chicken pox had begun to scab and her fever had abated. Hana watched the baby's hand steal toward her forehead in sleep, and she gently moved it back beneath the covers.

Downstairs again, Anton poured them each a brandy, and Hana sat down at the Bechstein and began a Bach fugue. Out the music poured, out into the autumn night, and then it was gone.

In the cold winter of 1939, the Germans came to Prague to stay. They said that Anton could no longer teach and that Hana could no longer play with the Symphony. Jewish children would not be permitted to attend the public schools, though Pavel and Heidi were too young to be affected by this.

Prisoners in their own home, Hana and Anton began to bicker. Hana found fault with the ashes carelessly tapped outside of ashtrays, and Anton complained he could not think for the sound of the piano that filled the house day in and day out. Often, even now in winter, he went outside to the garden and spent long hours sitting on a wrought-iron bench, smoking and staring at the broken brown stalks that reached through the snow.

To Hana, when she happened to glimpse him through a window, he looked like a man of only two dimensions, a man without hope. Her disappointment in his lethargy became a living thing within her, one that prodded and drove her, to create, create. She composed frantically, as if the wind that rattled the windows were something more threatening than mere wind, and she ignored even the children, who soon learned to avoid the conservatory when their mother sat before the Bechstein.

They had learned to avoid their father, too.

After these bouts of composing, Hana was strangely calm. She would go upstairs to her room and bathe, pin her hair up carefully and then put on a black evening dress, as if she were going out to perform. Out in the hall, she would call to the children, and then together they would go outside to the garden and coax Anton inside. A family once again, all were careful in their roles, mindful of both lines to be said and lines not to be crossed. Who are these people? Hana sometimes wondered. And what was it I once felt for them?

Hana's sister Raja and her husband Josef came to dinner, bearing black market bread and salamis beneath their coats. Josef was a jeweler, and he wore thick-lensed wire-rimmed glasses to compensate for his occupational nearsightedness. Raja, much younger than her husband, to whom she had been married for only a year, sported newly-hennaed hair, bright and unnatural in the dim light inside the house.

After dinner, they put the children to bed (Marya had left when Eichmann issued the edicts, in January) and then sat with brandies at one end of the dining room table. Hana watched her younger sister with an amused detachment, speaking little, though the others did not seem to notice.

Raja leaned closer across her brandy and lowered her voice. "Josef is going to get us American visas," she said. "He has a friend."

"Ha!" Anton spit out suddenly, and they all turned to him, wide-eyed. "You think that American visas will help us? You think that *Americans* will help us? We are Czechs—no, worse—we are Jews. The Americans do not care about us. The Americans do not wish to know we exist."

"Anton," Hana said, reaching to touch his hand. He would not look at her.

"Anton is right," Josef said in his quiet voice, running a finger around the rim of his glass. *E*, Hana thought, noting the height of the brandy. "But Czechs are not Germans. They will not allow the—hate—that is in Germany to happen here."

"One night, all over Germany, they broke all the glass," Raja said. "SS men, but boys and women too, they went into the Jewish section and they broke all the glass. No glass was left unbroken. They beat whatever Jews they found, and some they beat to death. I have heard this. It is true."

"Oh Raja!" Hana laughed. "'I have heard this? It is true?' Hitler said he did not want Czechoslovakia, and where is he now? Irena has always written weekly from Vienna, and now we have not heard from her since August. What we hear these days is *not* true. There *is* nothing true left in Prague, but most especially what we *hear* is not true."

"And every day we hear your music," Anton said. He said it quietly, as if to himself or perhaps not at all, and yet the effect was as if he had shouted it.

Hana stood, and walked to the piano in the adjoining room. "I will show you what is true," she said, and then she began to play what she had been creating throughout the winter.

While little of this was recorded in detail in Hana's notebooks, the drama opened itself before me as if it were a film and I its sole observer. And when Hana rose and went to the piano, I rose as well, and played.

The sound of the piano's strings is reinforced by a sound-board, a large sheet of wood that strengthens their vibrations. In addition, the modern piano's sound is controlled by three pedals: the damper, on the right, which causes the strings to continue to vibrate after the keys have been released; the *una corda*, on the left, which shifts the piano's action so that fewer strings are touched by the hammers; and the center *sostenuto*, which sustains a note just played even as another replaces it. Upright pianos often do not have a *sostenuto* pedal, an absence that also alters a tone's inevitable decay after it is sustained. "Move along! Move along!" urges the upright piano, a decidedly twentieth-century vehicle.

Research now suggests that a talent for playing a certain instrument, or for seeing things a certain way, is genetic. The entire science of genetics bases its premises on the thesis that we are products of our parents, that it is nature and not nurture that determines who and what we are.

My father was among the men who pored over a map of Japan and decided: *Hiroshima, Nagasaki.* While genetics suggests that I pay this heritage its due, I prefer to believe I have eluded its grasp. Instead, I am left to imagine the horror my father wrought.

My mother was delicate, and she died young, of tuberculosis, a disease that by 1965 was rare enough to be noteworthy. My mother's name was Katherine, a name I for some reason looked up in *6000 Names for Your Baby* the last time I was in the bookstore.

Katherine, it said. *(Greek): pure.*

Leon, my father's name, means "brave lion," which suggests that, genetically speaking, I am a pure, brave lion.

I much prefer the note for Anna in the same book: "Full of grace, mercy, and prayer." And among its many derivatives is Hana, which is, of course, mere coincidence.

In November, I switch my before-dinner drink from gin-and-tonic to rum-and-Coke. I'm not much of a drinker, but Paul likes a martini when he gets home from work and I usually join him.

After more than twenty-five years of marriage, routines seem as much a part of oneself as any genetic code. And so when Paul comes home on that November day each year when I've switched my drink, he says, "I see it's suddenly winter again," and, as always, he is right.

Because suddenly, it *was* winter. That is how it happens in New Mexico, from summer to winter with no interlude in between. In New York state, where I have also lived, there is fall, a season that allows one to become accustomed to darkness and cold once again. It was fall when I met Paul at Cornell, and so it is a season I have longed for ever since.

Cornell sits on a hill high above Lake Cayuga, its meandering roads and paths intersecting sudden gorges that, like those in Los Alamos, are startling in their depth. The fraternity houses are at the northern end of the campus, on the road that spools away to lands that still hold farms and sometimes long stretches without them.

Paul belonged to a Jewish fraternity, but, because I am not Jewish, it was not a distinction I made at the time. I have since come to believe that it is these groups themselves that somehow enforce their separateness—all the while insisting it is its opposite they desire. Perhaps there is a security in staying with those most like one, just as there is a perception that those who are not have something to which one should aspire.

I myself was at Cornell that weekend with a young man whose mother had gone to Vassar with my own. The mother lived in Irondequoit, a wealthy suburb of Rochester, and I was studying at the Rochester Institute of Music. It was Homecoming Weekend at Cornell and the son, apparently, was desperate for a date. This was in 1968, one of the last years during which such things would seem to matter.

He was tall and gangly and unfortunately beset with bad skin, and, try as I might, his name has disappeared too far into my memory to ever be recalled. He met me at the bus station in Ithaca, and he was driving a new, metallic green Mustang convertible. I remember the car, and its creamy white leather seats, and I remember complacent cows watching us from the sides of a gently winding highway, but I do not recall a thing we said to each other.

I stayed at a sorority house filled with women my own

age with whom I could find nothing in common. They knew I went to the Institute, though, and led me proudly to their badly tuned upright, demanding Beatles' songs while they drank Screwdrivers and chain-smoked Larks and Newports.

The football game was not memorable, though the autumn colors against a bright blue sky and the singular smell of burning leaves were. After the game my date and I walked across the campus slightly apart from the group I assumed we were a part of, not even bothering to forge a conversation where no commonality lay. When we arrived at his fraternity house, where the party would be, we made no attempt to stay together.

Perhaps it's the nature of the only child that makes her an observer, a watcher, a percher on the edge of things. Whatever the case, I was content to sit on a couch in the corner, nursing a long-gone-warm gin-and-tonic. Then one of the sorority girls spotted me and pulled me to an out-of-tune upright disarmingly similar to the previous night's; I remember a moment of disorientation when I wondered if it weren't the same instrument. They didn't care about the tuning, of course; it was the semblance of accompaniment they were after, a background to their atonal singing.

When Paul sat down next to me on the bench and set down a fresh gin-and-tonic, I was playing "Michelle" for the third time. "You're what's-his-name's date," he said, and I nodded. "I'm his roommate. Paul Kramer."

"Anna Holtz." I stopped playing and took a sip of the drink. No one noticed; the singing continued, in all of its assorted keys.

"This will seem like a stupid question," he said, "but you're not related to Major General Leon Holtz?"

"I'm his daughter."

"Wow," he said, in the parlance of the day. It belied his enthusiasm, which was, as befitted a graduate student in nuclear physics, considerable.

So I could say I owe my marriage to my father, although that would not be precisely true. While Paul was suitably awed by my pedigree, it would not have been enough to sustain his interest. I am certain that it was I Paul fell in love with, a love I am rather fond of recalling now, these many years later, when it seems to have resolutely settled into something quite other. This is not to say Paul and I are not contented with each other, or with our life together. It's rather that, or so it seemed to us at the time, we were once in love. It is only when such things are over that we realize what it was we once had, although we are unable to recreate the emotions that briefly sustained us. What is left rings hollow, like the many instruments that are now found only in museums: generated in enthusiasm but disappointing in their manifestation. It is difficult to know whether the failure of imagination occurred at the inception, or some time later. It is easy to look away, and move on to the next exhibit.

My father took to Paul at once. By 1969, he had retired from active duty, and spent his days tending a rather spectacular rose garden in the backyard of his house. This house, in which I had grown up, was one of the nicest ones then in Los Alamos, set far back on a road that wound through ponderosa, and edged by a deep-walled red rock canyon.

While my father showed Paul his roses, I walked down the path to the canyon's edge. It was June, a hot month, but a coolness seemed to rise from the chasm, and a pair of hawks floated lazily at the level of my eyes. On the far side of the canyon, new houses were sprouting in a subdivision—aluminum-sided ranches surrounded by the stumps of the ponderosas razed to make room for them.

This was during the uranium boom, when enterprising businessmen grouped together and leased land from the Indian tribes, then hired cheap Indian labor to dig the ore out. Uranium was everywhere in the four states region, a coincidence whose providence was not lost on my father, who was one of the men getting rich.

At dinner, he and Paul discussed fission and the more recently tested theory of fusion. They speculated about the size of rings of destruction, of fail-safe zones and of zones of immediate death. My father mentioned how when they had begun testing, the birds had fallen out of the sky. As scientists, they were disassociated from the realities of these statistics, but I was not a scientist and found I could not eat my dinner.

When the bomb was dropped on Hiroshima, I once read, the flowered patterns of women's black-and-white kimonos were burned onto their skin. This is because white repels the bomb's heat while black absorbs it. When I got up to make coffee for my father and Paul that evening, I noticed for the first time the pattern of my mother's kitchen curtains, the curtains that had hung over her sink for as long as I could remember, a pattern of large white flowers against a red background, a pattern, I suddenly decided, that my mother felt was representative of far more than she had ever said.

But my mother never said much, not to my father, and not to me. I had learned when I was young not to question, but I had also learned that sometimes my mother would speak, as if I were not there, and that, if I was very quiet, I would learn some of the things I longed to know.

It was often late at night, when my mother talked to me. We were both prone to insomnia, and would leave our beds for the safer haven the kitchen seemed to provide. I now believe that the conversations that matter, the ones that we remember, the ones where words can actually express what we mean, are those that take place late at night, in kitchens, or in places equally extraordinary in their innocuousness.

The night after President Kennedy was shot, a Saturday, I found my mother at the kitchen table, drinking tea. She favored dark China black or Oolong or Formosa, laced with light cream and a touch of sugar, and she would brew it in a chipped white pot that was stamped *Occupied Japan* on its bottom.

I poured myself a glass of milk and joined her at the table, and then saw that she was crying. She cried soundlessly, my mother, and the only evidence that she was were the wet channels of tears on her cheeks that she made no move to brush away.

"It's the children for whom I'm crying," she said. This was how my mother phrased things, formally, a tendency that I have perhaps inherited along with others more obvious. "It's not just that they're fatherless now, it's how their father died, in slow motion pictures they're doomed to watch again and again."

I, too, though at fifteen no longer a child, watched those films again and again. They were burned onto my brain as if the chemicals themselves had etched them there, slow motion images of a man, John F. Kennedy, alive and smiling and waving one moment, and slumped, bleeding, in his wife's lap the next.

"Every time it seems things cannot possibly get worse," my mother said, "they do."

A little over a year later, my mother was dead. The refrain of a song from *Carousel* repeated itself, over and over, as I sat in the front row of a crowded Fuller Lodge for her funeral; my mother had loved *Carousel*, as she had most musicals, but that is not why those were the words that day. Rather, I would like to believe, they meant that in death my mother had finally discovered hope.

Hope was not something that Hana Weissova thought of any-more. In July of 1941, the Nuremberg Laws, which effectively reduced Jews to sub-human status, were extended to those living in Czechoslovakia, and Jacob Edelstein, the leader of Prague's Jewish community, began to study the possibility of ghettoizing Prague's Jews, a desperate measure he saw as their best chance of survival. In August, Raja and Josef moved in with Hana and Anton, and in September, Anton's parents, from the Bohemian town of Holîce, followed.

Hana's parents were with her sister Irena in Vienna, or at least had been the last time she had written. In that last letter Irena had said that they were thinking of going to Shanghai. Perhaps they had. Perhaps that was why the weekly letters had ceased.

Her own letters to Irena had not been returned, a good sign, Hana told herself. She wondered if there was a symphony in Shanghai (Irena played the viola), and what the climate was like; anything would be better for their mother's rheumatism than Vienna's dampness.

Every morning, Anton and Josef joined the line outside the American Embassy. Each wore on his arm the two yellow triangles, one inverted against the other, that indicated they were Jews. The gentile citizens of Prague avoided not just them but in particular their eyes, as if to deny their very existence and hence their humanity.

And every evening, Anton and Josef returned home empty-handed. Hana would see their slow approach along the walk below the window by her piano, and every day, it seemed, their feet dragged more and more. Every day their chins hung lower toward their chests, and every day they brought with them into the house a heavy emptiness, an emptiness that even the piano's music was reluctant to encroach upon.

So Hana would close the piano when she heard the front door open and instead would sit in the silent conservatory. She would listen as Raja, Mother Weissova, and the children came down the stairs from the nursery, hear the men greet the children with false heartiness. "Come into the kitchen," Mother Weissova would say, "and see what we've made," and then Hana would hear the group recede to the other side of the house.

This is when Raja would join her. Hana was the oldest of the three sisters and Raja the youngest, separated by Irena and four years. She was not yet twenty, Raja, this summer of 1941, but her face had grown lines, and the henna had faded from her curly hair so that it was once again merely brown.

Raja had always been the lively one, the one to play practical jokes, to forget curfews, to sing for no reason, to believe in the joyfully unexpected and hence to receive it. Not musical like her sisters, her talents lay rather in a capacity for happiness, for a giving of herself for which one was always grateful. Where Hana and Irena tended to be inward and moody, Raja was outgoing and always smiling. She had often got on Hana's nerves.

She was still optimistic, in spite of all that had happened. "No visas today," she would say, folding herself carelessly into an upholstered chair near the fireplace. "Tomorrow, perhaps." Hana no longer argued with her about this, no longer said, *There will never be visas*, because it was always as if Raja had not heard, as if, even, Hana had not said it. Instead, she became an echo. "Yes," she would say. "Tomorrow, perhaps."

"Pavel is learning to read," Raja said this night. "The Grimm, which he is always having me read to him—he read some out loud himself, today."

"He has probably got it memorized," Hana said. "He has heard it often enough."

Raja leaned forward, her hands etching her thoughts before her words. "Yes, that is what I thought, too, at first, so I made a little test. I opened the book randomly, and I put my hand over the drawing, so he would not see which story it was."

"Which story was it?" Hana asked. As if that would somehow explain things.

"'Rapunzel,'" Raja answered. "'Because her beauty so frightened the witch, the witch locked her in a tower, so deep in the woods no one should ever find her.'"

Hana shivered. "How does that one end again? I've forgotten."

Raja laughed. "Oh Hana, you know how it ends: 'They lived happily ever after.' That is how it always ends."

Yes, thought Hana. It is a fairy tale, after all.

That is what the Kennedys had been to us, a fairy tale. Even my sad mother had allowed herself to be enchanted by it, and so its abrupt and horrible ending must have seemed to her as if she had suddenly turned the page to find herself in quite another story.

My mother always went to the piano at those times. Perhaps that's why I've sent Hana there, made it the refuge for her it was for my mother. Hana's long fingers are, like my mother's, unadorned, and she tilts her head slightly to the right as she plays, as if she hears the music's suggestion a moment before she reproduces it on the keys.

I have never pretended to possess my mother's talent, and I cannot hope to have Hana's. I am, unlike them, destined to mediocrity, a piano teacher, a woman whose life is small and whose dissonances are never heard.

It is the soloist's responsibility to perform a single part, a part not duplicated by other instruments or voices. The solo is meant to emphasize the individual qualities of the instrument for which it is intended rather than its contribution to the total effect. While it is often the case, the solo is not written to showcase its performer.

The piano is used mainly as a solo instrument, and so the

pianist tends to be a solitary sort. The pianist, unlike other members of an orchestra, sits alone behind her massive instrument, of which there is only one. Eighteen first violins and sixteen second, twelve violas, ten cellos, eight double basses: this is the bowed string section, and other instruments are similarly grouped. Even the percussionists stand together, there at the back, behind the horns, but the pianist, with her piano, is a section of her own.

While it is this singularity that initially attracts beginners to the piano, it is also what ultimately drives them away. Few people can devote their lives to a passion that marginalizes them. But those who do find that this marginalization is part of the passion.

My 3:30 Monday student is Karen Maisel. Karen's father is a mid-level administrator at the Labs, and her mother a third-grade teacher at the elementary school. Karen is an only child.

At ten, she is gawky and shy, all arms and legs and avoidance of eye contact. Her obligatory jeans and white t-shirts hang from her as if she were fashioned from coat hangers instead of skin and bone, and her brown bangs fall over her glasses, round tortoise-shell horn-rims whose thick lenses attest to myopia.

Even with the glasses, Karen leans and squints toward the music. Her hands play the notes exactly as they are written, but with nothing behind them, as is usually the case with children of unremarkable talent. Sometimes, after our lesson and before the arrival of Curtis Simon at five, we will sit at my kitchen table awaiting Karen's mother. Karen's hands will play with the edges of a placemat, or turn the sugar bowl around and around in careful quarter turns, and her chin will be tucked so low her muttered responses disappear unheard.

I would like Karen Maisel to make the mysterious leap from rote to music, but I am at a loss as to how to proceed. The literature suggests practice, but there is something else besides, a moment when the music, in its course from page to key, passes through the pianist, becomes imbued, colored by the pianist's essence, and is so transformed.

My own teacher, when I was ten, was my mother, and she taught this lesson early and well. But I realize now that she did not teach me with words but by example: I would hear her rendition of a piece and then my own and the difference was electric.

I cannot, of course, hope to give the same example to Karen. Unlike my mother's, my playing is pedestrian and unremarkable, a faithful but uninspired reproduction of the notes on the page.

This was not the case, however, with Hana Weissova's sonatas. No music before or since has communicated itself to me as Hana's did; I was, in fact, haunted by it. Nights, I lay in bed, awake while my husband slept oblivious by my side, arpeggios and chord progressions playing unbidden in my mind. Pale figures danced wordlessly in unknown rooms. Colors swirled: the gauzy green of a woman's gown, the deep maroon of velvet curtains tied with gold tassels. Sometimes I was certain I heard voices: my mother's, as clearly as if she were in the room with me; and Hana Weissova's, absurdly, as I could not know that voice, and yet it was familiar nonetheless.

The music, too, was colored, and, lying in bed, I could hear and see it as if Hana Weissova sat at her Bechstein playing for me alone. Hana, too, was alone, the solitary figure that all pianists ultimately are.

I was often alone, as a child. Other children in the neighborhood could be seen playing games I could not fathom: tiptoeing single file through the alleys behind the houses; racing along the roads on squat bicycles with high, unwieldy handlebars; swinging bats at softballs in the playground or in the middle of the street. Of course, I did once have a friend. But she has been dead for such a long time now, it is difficult for me to remember what it was like.

I stayed home for my mother. It was not that she wanted me to, or even that she needed me; it was rather that that was where I wished to be. Did I know she would die young, retreat into herself long before that? I think not, but it was nonetheless with her I preferred to be.

Still, we lived separate, solitary existences within the same house. I tiptoed when I moved about; I opened and closed doors as quietly as I could; I worried that the toilet's flush was too jarring a sound and often put off peeing until the pain was nearly unbearable.

My mother moved through the house like a ghost. I read a great deal, curled in chairs or sprawled on rugs, and my mother would sometimes appear, soundlessly and suddenly. "You're reading," she would say, a statement rather than a question, but I would say yes, and go on to tell her about the book.

My mother would tilt her head slightly to the right as I spoke, the way she did when she was playing. She seemed to be trying to make sense of the words, to translate them into something she could somehow understand. But when I finished talking, she would say only, "That's very nice, dear," and then she would leave the room as she had entered it, so that I was sometimes unsure she had really been there at all.

I had, though, lengthy imagined conversations with her. During these talks, she would reach out to brush my hair from my face, or to touch my hand or shoulder, something she never did, in life. My imagined mother was both witty and wise, able to solve the most difficult problems in remarkably simple ways. She had a lovely, musical laugh, and bright dancing eyes that cherished me in their unwavering gaze. My imagined mother wished for me love, and fame, and fortune, and she was there at my side to share all these things, and more.

I have read that a propensity for melancholy may be genetic, though I have also read that it is a learned trait. Artists tend toward melancholy, as do the naturally solitary, the painfully shy.

My father was neither melancholy, nor solitary, nor shy. He was a serious and straightforward man—no-nonsense, one biographer has said—but also capable of unexpected laughter at a "good one," and backslapping camaraderie with the men with whom he worked.

My father adored my mother; I might even say he worshipped her. And yet it is clear to me, in retrospect, that he had no idea that the more expansive he grew, the more she shrunk. My mother's essence waned smaller and smaller, until, one winter, she was gone.

For Hana, it was another autumn. Jews from Bohemia and Moravia streamed into Prague, their home provinces having been declared off-limits to them.

The Germans showed a remarkable efficiency in moving large numbers of people from place to place. The final chilling degree of this efficiency would not be realized until after the war, but even in Prague, in the fall of 1941, it was something one could not help but nearly admire.

The large house became crowded with refugees. At first, it was relatives, but soon the connections were less clear, and farmers and peasants shared rooms with store clerks and bakers with whom they'd had nothing in common in their prior existences.

At the same time, food became more and more scarce. Mother Weissova, head now of a kitchen with too many cooks, improvised huge pots of broth stewed from whatever Raja managed to bring home. Rose petals from the garden were carefully saved to brew tea, and even leaves and twigs added substance and flavor to what otherwise would have been little more than boiled water.

Raja was often gone. Hana suspected that she was a member of the underground, but the one time she asked, Raja only laughed.

In early October, though, Raja came home and said they must prepare to leave at once. She told this to Hana while curled in her usual chair by the fireplace. Several Bohemian women sat in a far corner, patching clothes, and so Raja spoke in French.

"Leave?" Hana said, with a short laugh. "Leave and go

where? We are two young couples, two young children, and one old couple. We are too many people and there is nowhere for us to go. Here, at least, we are home."

"This will not be home much longer," Raja said, watching the Bohemian women, who had stopped talking and seemed to be listening. "*Parlez-vous Français?*" she said to them, and they laughed. Satisfied, or pretending to be, that they could not understand her, she went on. "You know Terezín? The old fortress?" Hana nodded. "They are making it into a camp, for the Jews of Prague."

"A camp?" Hana pictured an idyllic cabin, set by a lake, amid pines.

"A labor camp. The Germans are setting them up in all their occupied territories, places where they use Jews as slave labor." She paused. "I have heard worse," she said in a lower voice.

"What could be worse?" Hana laughed again, wondering if her laugh had ever been without this bitter edge.

Raja leaned forward and reached for Hana's hand. "I have heard that there are other camps, whose purpose is to kill Jews. I have heard that the Nazis are trying to find the most efficient way to do this."

Hana shivered. "Even the Nazis could not do such a thing," she said, and found she could not seem to breathe. "Where have you heard this?"

Raja let go of her hand and sat back again. "Please do not ask me these things, Hana. If you do not know, you cannot say."

"I would not say!"

"I know you would not mean to," Raja said. "But if you do not know, you cannot. Please, Hana. We must leave."

Hana looked around the room, looked beyond it, picturing the house's other rooms, its garden, its proud stone façade. She pictured her children, now grown so thin, her husband and his haunted eyes, her mother-in-law and her accusing ones. And Father Weiss, nearly always in bed now—it was not possible.

"It is not possible," she said.

"Hana—"

"Your information may be wrong."

"My information is not wrong."

"Raja." Now it was Hana who reached across for her sister's hand. "They would not survive. They are not well. You and I—we are the only strong ones." She splayed her hand, its bony fingers. "And even we grow thin. No. At least here we are home."

Raja nodded slowly. "Josef and I will go, though. Two fewer mouths to feed, and when we arrive somewhere safe, we will send for you."

"You have talked to Josef about this then?"

"Josef is my husband."

"And you have talked to him?"

Raja smiled. "Tonight, I will. We must go. I wish you would at least consider it, Hana. Please."

"All right," Hana said. But she knew she would not.

When Raja and Josef left the next morning, Hana was not with the others in the front entry hall to see them off. She sat instead at her piano, but she did not begin to play until they passed beneath her window. Then she took up a Mozart minuet, sprightly and free. She saw Raja pause and look toward the window, and then quickly move on. Raja's head was held high, and her hand firmly grasped Josef's elbow. Hana watched the familiar backs of their heads grow smaller and smaller, until they rounded the corner across the street, and disappeared.

I still have not found Raja, a 1946 note in Hana's diary reads. *I believe that is cause for hope. I only wish that I had learned to pray, or that I believed in the power of prayer.*

I, too, never learned to pray. But, for some reason, I do believe in something. I believe, for example, that when I sit alone playing my piano, my mother hears. I believe that when I play Hana Weissova's sonatas, Hana's spirit somehow guides me.

My father was a man of science. "I'm from Missouri," he'd always say. "Show me." But my mother was of another sensibility, a woman who understood the very different empiricism of music. My mother, I have begun to understand, knew that music, in its way, was the highest form of prayer.

Like any discipline, music has a language and vocabulary that is uniquely its own. Musical sounds, for example, have four properties—pitch, dynamics, tone color, and duration— and it is these properties that distinguish it from other sounds.

Pitch is the highness or lowness one hears, a specific frequency which in music is called a tone. The distance between two tones is called an interval, and chords, groupings of notes played simultaneously, are comprised of these intervals.

The loudness or softness of music is called dynamics.

Composers indicate dynamics in their notation with Italian terms, from *pianissimo*—very soft, to *fortissimo*—very loud. The original name of the piano, in fact, was *pianoforte*, a word which indicated the instrument's unique dynamic capacity.

Tone color refers to a quality of sound, the certain timbre created by an instrument. A trumpet, for example, is said to have a brilliant timbre, while a cello or an oboe is more mellow, and often more dark in color.

Duration, unlike the other properties of musical sound, is a relative term; it indicates how long each tone lasts in relation to the others in a particular piece. In this relative way of viewing the duration of my life, I have already lived longer than my mother, while the time she was a part of mine comprises barely a third of its duration.

In terms of human history, my forty-some years make no sound at all; and, in terms of geological history, I do not even exist. Pitch, dynamics, and tone color pale beside the impact of duration, but without them musical sound would be no different from any other.

It is that difference that makes music a haven quite unlike others; it is that difference that creates in music a place where one's self ceases to matter, or even, in a way, to exist.

Nuclear physics has its own language as well. Physicists talk of critical mass, fissionable material, implosion, detonation. In the Los Alamos of the early 1940s the language also included strategy, preemptive strikes, and "the possibility of heavy casualties," as well as "the importance of overwhelming surprise."

That I define my father in terms of this language should

not be an overwhelming surprise. Unlike my feelings about my mother, my thoughts about my father were always clear and direct, a reflection, after all, of the man himself. My father was, in his own choice words of praise, "a man of action." He was a "quick study," "decisive," "straight-forward," "authoritative."

The man I knew at home as I grew up was not at odds with the man the histories and biographies have drawn. If a decision needed to be made, it was my father who would make it, just as, if a line needed to be drawn, he would draw it.

I was never of a rebellious nature. The bounds of my existence were very clearly marked, and it did not occur to me to cross them. Even when I became old enough to wonder about some of my father's decisions, I did not second-guess him. I was not fissionable material, potentially imploding upon detonation, but I was, quite possibly, the result of a strategy that was preemptive and hence left no margin for error.

My earliest memory of my father is a winter one. I am five, and he is kneeling at my feet in our front yard's snow, strapping cross-country skis to my heavy boots.

What I am seeing is the top of my father's head—the dark, slicked-back hair, the tops of his protruding ears, the brown fuzziness of his leather bomber jacket's collar. I see his breath, too, translucent question marks that come up over his forehead and then dissipate into the blueness of the sky.

Behind me, I hear my mother open the front door, and I try to turn, but only succeed in twisting the upper half of my body. My mother, wrapped in a navy blue cardigan that is far too big and that I have never seen before, leans on the doorjamb and twiddles her fingers at me: a wave. I wave back, mittened. My father looks up, sees her, jumps up and runs to the door in what seems like two incredibly long strides. Rooted to my skis, I remain half-turned, watching as my father kisses my mother's forehead, touches her elbow, and guides her inside. Then, closing the door behind him, he's back, strapping on his own skis and handing me two sawed-off poles. "Okay," he says. "Let's go."

It does not occur to me to say I don't know how to ski, that he has never shown me how. My father has said, "Let's go," and go I must, and go I do, in short mincing steps and then longer gliding ones to catch up with him. He never looks back to see if I am there, because he knows I am, and I know I must not disappoint him.

At first, I stay in the twin tracks my father's skis have traced for me, but as I become more accustomed to my feet's lengthy extensions I move parallel to him, although still behind. Under my skis the snow repeats the same soothing sound over and over, *sh-sh, sh-sh*, its smoothness so reassuring that I fall into it as if we were one.

We ski at the edge of the canyon, and we ski for a very long time. We encounter no one, and we never say a word to each other. It is only hindsight that tells me that what I experienced that afternoon may well have been my only moments of pure joy.

S<small>TUDIES</small> of manic depression indicate that *Two*
the illness precludes any emotional middle
ground. Either the patient is manic—on a high—or
depressed, with no halfway point to temper her.

Other studies now suggest that there are a few self-cured
manic depressives, who have found that halfway point and
tethered themselves there so firmly that both elation and
melancholy seem vague memories not even their own. Self-
cured manic depressives steer a careful course along a deceptively smooth surface, allowing themselves neither happiness
nor sadness. One often feels, in discourse with these people,
that one is getting only a polished veneer, but also that, were
that veneer to be stripped, there would be nothing beneath
it. Self-cured manic depressives protect themselves so well
that they have lost their cores along with their highs and lows.

Core, of course, is yet another word in the language of nuclear physics, a word often used in conjunction with the adjectives supercooled, or superheated.

I came across the article discussing self-cured manic depressives in my dentist's waiting room. The only surprise in it for me was the implication that one would have had the highs and the lows before one cured oneself.

I do not recall a time I had not firmly tethered myself to that halfway point, a place that is both safe and unremarkable. No tricks of light on water for me: I stand safely on the shore, watching.

Perhaps that is why my playing is doomed to mediocrity. Perhaps in order to convey emotion in music, one must experience the emotions oneself. I do not recall my mother, however, displaying emotion of any kind. Rather, there was only her vague lethargy—except when she played.

When my mother played, the music took on shape and color. Music was the place where my mother could allow her emotions to surface, and it is curious that I cannot do the same. It is possible that I am so afraid of what those emotions will reveal that I cannot allow even their possibility. But how can I be afraid of what I have never felt? Or is it possible that I *did* once know elation, or sorrow, an elation or sorrow I can no longer recall, but which served as a warning that such feelings were dangerous?

After skiing that afternoon, my father and I arrived home as the sun set behind the ponderosas. My father unstrapped my skis and then his own, and leaned them up against the house. I was still filled with that peculiar sense that I am hesitant to name, a sense that all was right with the world, that nothing could ever hurt me so long as my father was there.

We went into the house and my father called out for my mother. When she did not answer, he said, "Perhaps she's upstairs" and went to look.

I stood alone in the front hall, still wrapped in coat and muffler, mittens and hat. My heavy boots dripped onto the tiled floor, but the front hall was peculiarly quiet, the ticking of the clock unusually loud against this silence. I concentrated on each tick, so that the sound became the only thing. I knew how to count to ten, and so I counted ten ticks and then started over, I don't know how many times. It was as if I were not in my own familiar home but somewhere else entirely, as if I were not even myself but had ceased to exist. I would not move. I stood, and I counted ten ticks, and then I counted again.

When my father came back down the stairs, my mother was behind him. And that is where this memory ends.

Though Raja had warned her, Hana was nonetheless surprised when the SS came. They came for the men, they said, strong young men who would help to build a camp where they could live.

Anton left in October. That fall was as cold as the previous fall had been warm, and he left bundled in several layers of sweaters, his warm overcoat, a muffler and hat. Hana stood at the door and adjusted the muffler at his throat, the throat of this stranger who was her husband. "I will see you soon," she said. "We will all see you soon." Anton did not answer.

Hana stood on her toes and whispered that she loved him. She kissed his ear, and then his cheek, and then his lips, and said again, "I love you, Anton. Remember that." But Anton did not answer, and then he was gone.

The winter was long and cold. In addition, firewood was scarce, and by December, Hana began assessing her furniture to decide what was expendable.

Because she was always cold, she bundled up the children, who then complained of being too hot. Mother Weissova had brought the herbs and vegetables from the garden into the kitchen before the frost, and they grew in pots and pans on the counters and windowsills. Father Weiss, meanwhile, grew weaker and thinner, and Hana took to sitting with him in the waning hours of the afternoons. She had never really known this man, her father-in-law, but now they talked for hours, the winter's thin light filtered by the room's gauzy curtains.

His name was Petr, and he had been a shopkeeper. Their town had not been large, and so he had stocked both usual and unusual items—fabric and flour, tiny wooden Swiss clocks and bottles of French wine. He knew all of his customers well, knew their histories and their families, knew who was going through a difficult time and so would say, "I will put this on your account, correct?" Even now, in Prague, former customers came to visit him, Jews and non-Jews, the latter sometimes whispering to Hana in the foyer that the fate of Jews should not befall Petr Weiss, who did not seem Jewish at all.

But it should befall other Jews? Hana thought but did not say. She was suddenly aware of the dichotomy, of her Jewishness, a fact to which she had previously paid no more attention than the color of her hair or her eyes. One afternoon she mentioned this to Father Weiss, propped up against his many pillows, his strong features cast in relief on his too-thin face, his still-thick grey hair combed neatly back from his forehead by his wife that morning.

"We are not any different," Hana said to him. "I do not understand."

Father Weiss smiled, and patted her hand where it lay beneath his on the comforter. "Ah, Hana," he said, "but we *are* different. We are God's chosen people."

"Biblical bunk," Hana said. "Who in the twentieth century would believe such a thing?"

"I do not disagree with you that the Bible is, as you call it, 'bunk,' but the Jews, because of that bunk, *are* different. Think of it, Hana: For 5000 years, against all kinds of odds, our people have persevered. We have been exiled, vilified, forbidden to worship our God, scapegoated, and sometimes murdered, but still we have chosen to be Jewish. A lesser people would have compromised long ago."

Hana held his cup to his lips while he took a sip of tea, then set it down again on the bed table. "All right," she said, "that is all true. But my question is what is it that we would be compromising? What is it that Jews must cling to so tenaciously that they will die for it?"

Petr smiled. "Why, our Jewishness, Hana. The very thing that sets us apart."

"I don't understand. Why do we want to be set apart?"

"Because if we don't do it, others will. We say we are special, that we are 'chosen,' before *they* say we are wicked, purveyors of their Satan."

"But why be apart at all? Why not simply be like the

others, so they will not be tempted to single us out?"

"They will always single us out, Hana. We may marry non-Jews who in turn marry non-Jews. Our Jewishness may become a mere fraction of our genetic whole, but it will always be there." He raised a cupped hand to his mouth in the manner of a secret sharer. "'Have you not heard Petr Weiss had a Jewish great-grandmother on his father's side?' they will say. They will whisper behind their hands, watch you for those telltale moves that prove your Jewishness. Have you not heard that Hitler's maternal grandmother may have been Jewish?"

"Yes, and I find that hard to understand as well."

"They *wish* to understand him, Hana; that is why they make these explanations. All humans wish to understand, and when things defy their understanding they will seek answers in folklore or rumor. The Gentiles have been taught that a Jew is a certain way, and evidence of this way is proof of Jewishness. It might as well be science."

"But we are no different!"

"Hana, Hana. We *are*. We are tenacious and we are clever. We are learned and we care for one another. A Jew always knows another Jew, and will turn to him first, in need. *Tzedaka* makes us different, and history. We cannot pretend to be like them, Hana, because we are not."

Hana looked across the bed to the window, its panes etched in frost, then back to her father-in-law's Aryan blue eyes. "I don't want to be different," she said.

"I think that is not true, Hana. I think you want to be very different. It is just that you do not want your Jewishness to be what makes you so."

It was so true it startled her. Why hadn't she seen this

herself? She rose, and smiled down at him. "I'm going down-stairs now, Father. What shall I play for you today?"

He smiled back, meeting her eyes so that she knew they understood each other. "There is that lovely Hebrew song, '*Dodi Li*,' do you know it?" He hummed the first five notes.

"Father," Hana said. "We played that at our wedding. Instead of the Mendelssohn, remember?"

"Why yes," Petr said. "So you did."

"*Dodi Li*"? How would I know the name of a Hebrew song? I had even heard the notes Father Weiss hummed, a haunt-ing and familiar melody I was certain was new to me.

The conversation about Jewishness I recognized as a vari-ation of one I'd had with my mother-in-law, so perhaps the song was one she'd mentioned as well. I went into the kitchen and called her, then, as the phone rang, visualized her making her way through her North Buffalo flat to answer.

"'*Dodi Li*,'" she said, and then she hummed it as well. "Perhaps you heard it at someone's wedding—it's often played. What made you think of it?"

The question caught me off guard, and I realized all at once how much time I'd been spending daydreaming Hana Weissova's life. I told my mother-in-law bits of music often came into my head unbidden, but that since this one had come with a distinctively Hebrew name, I'd known at once whom to call.

"And so, how is my son?" she asked, apparently satisfied by my answer, and I told her some more lies, all the while wondering how I'd come to be obsessed by a woman whom I'd never known.

The resting place at the end of a musical phrase is called a cadence. Some cadences are unresolved or ask a question, and are called incomplete; others meet the first's expectations or answer its question and so are called complete. The ear demands complete cadence: imagine a song that ends one note too soon, or one note too late.

A melody—*Dodi Li*, for example—is comprised of sequences of incomplete and complete cadences, and in an extended piece of music, these repetitions and variations can be recognized as the piece's theme. In music, every question has an answer; every expectation is met and completed.

It is only in life that such resolutions are not possible: Expectation is one thing, completion quite another.

It is difficult to talk to Paul about music, but I sometimes try nonetheless. "What do you think of the Shostakovich?" I'll ask him when I return to the den after playing it. Paul is leaned far back in his recliner, reading the Lab news in the *Monitor*.

"Hm?" he says, without looking up.

"The Shostakovich. 'Six Preludes and Fugues.' It's difficult to play, but some people say it's boring to hear."

"Boring?" Paul still doesn't look up. "It wasn't boring, honey. Play it again. I liked it."

I don't want to play it again, but I've been trained to be dutiful. This time I try to listen as well as play, but one can't do both at the same time. I recall that Bartok claimed that he found one of Shostakovich's symphonic themes so silly that he decided to parody it. On a whim, I close the score and try a parody myself: consonance, break, dissonance; consonance, break, dissonance.

"My God," Paul calls from the other room. "That's *awful*. What are you playing?"

"Nothing," I answer, closing the piano. But I'm oddly satisfied, as if some bothersome question has suddenly been answered.

"Again," my mother said, and I repeated the intermezzo. I knew it by heart, by rote, and I'd steal looks at her, where she stood clutching the curtain and gazing out toward the canyon. When I finished, I stopped, the silence lifting from the piano to fill the room.

When this silence reached my mother, she would say, "Again." She never moved, and I played the intermezzo over and over. Dusk fell, and then dark, but we lit no light and my mother never moved, and after a while I started over without her prompt, so that the intermezzo became a rondo, a circular piece that never ends, but only returns to its own beginning, again and again.

I do not recall my mother having friends. Certainly, I have no friends, not of the secret-sharing variety, at any rate. Of course, Los Alamos is the kind of town that seems to preclude friendships of what I imagine to be the usual sort. People are secretive, but they are also self-involved; the percentage of geniuses in Los Alamos is many times the national average.

The percentage of suicides is also disproportionately

high. There's an oft-repeated bit of local folklore that says that when someone decides to throw himself off the gorge bridge, everyone else will go to measure his velocity. I do not know if this is precisely true, but its metaphor is telling.

My best friend in high school, Barbara Stewart, killed herself, but she did not throw herself off the gorge bridge. Her velocity was of a different sort: she stopped eating.

I'd never been much of an eater myself, and so at first I didn't notice. But Barbara began to demand notice. "Look at my fat fingers," she'd say, and when I looked I'd see skin hung on bone. "Isn't she stunning?" she'd say of Twiggy, an emaciated model whose enormous eyes were painted round with eyelashes, and then, "Do I look like her?" She'd cut her hair short and boyish by then, and painted on the same lashes, but where Twiggy had a glow Barbara had a pallor, a blue tinge to her skin that I did not think entirely unattractive.

When her parents finally put her in the hospital, Barbara weighed 74 pounds. She was still strong enough to rip out her IV and then tape it back on so that it looked as if it were connected.

The last time I visited her before she died, she said, "I'm so fat." She weighed 57 pounds. Her parents had her body cremated, and I have no idea what they did with her ashes, which perhaps weighed little enough that Barbara finally achieved her dream.

The children were so thin that when the SS came, in April, to tell them that they would all be moved to the camp at Theresienstadt, Hana was relieved. It would, after all, be in the Nazis' best interests to keep their workers well-fed, though it was difficult to imagine what a three- and five-year-old might work at.

Father and Mother Weiss were moved first. Hundreds of trucks arrived in Prague to transport the elderly, along with those the Jewish Council deemed privileged. The latter included doctors, politicians, artisans, and musicians, though because Hana had not been regularly employed since Pavel was born, she was not among them.

It was raining the morning the trucks came, a hard steady rain that had begun the afternoon before and showed no sign of letting up soon. The trucks had canvas awnings over their beds, but the rain blew in through the sides and backs, and people jostled for positions toward the fronts, where it was a little drier.

Through the conservatory window, Hana watched the soldiers loading old men and women into the transports. The soldiers were young, their faces impassive, but they seemed kind and concerned, often assisting women up the step by holding their elbows. Aside from the soldiers and the people lined up waiting to be loaded, the street was deserted: no children playing; no women rushing toward unknown but important destinations; no men gathered at the corner park's benches to argue the latest turn of events. Pink blossoms danced in the rain and then fell to the street to be lost in its black gloss. Everything but the blossoms appeared to be monochromatic, a distinction Hana would later recall as the last time she saw color until after the war.

When Hana heard the sounds of Mother Weissova assisting Father Weiss slowly down the stairs, she left her post and went to help. Although it was April, and warm, he was dressed in his overcoat, muffler, and black hat, his hands gloved, his overshoes securely fastened over his polished oxfords. Mother Weissova wore her mink coat and matching hat, elegant black heels, and a simple black dress. She was, Hana suddenly realized, much younger than her husband, 45 to his 65, and this morning she looked younger still. Her black hair was pinned back into a tidy twist beneath her hat, and she held Petr's elbow firmly, her gaze focused down the stairs before her.

Hana took Petr's other elbow and together the three descended to the foyer and then stopped. Petr breathed heavily, but still managed to say what a lucky man he was to be attended by two lovely young women. The women exchanged glances but laughed at the same time.

Heidi and Pavel appeared, and Mother Weissova knelt to straighten collars, to lick her finger and press awkward strands of hair into place, then at last to kiss each cheek and hug each child. "You are the man now," she told Pavel, who deepened his voice to reply, "Yes, Ma'am," with such solemnity that all laughed again.

Mother Weissova turned to Hana, and the women embraced and kissed formally, then more intimately. "You will give Anton my love?" Hana said.

"Of course," Mother answered. "And before too long, we will all be together again."

Hana turned to Father Weiss, the man she'd grown to cherish above all others these last six months. "Father," she began, but then could find no words to continue and so embraced him silently, tears starting in her eyes. Father Weiss scolded, "No need to cry, Hana," and she nodded, though they both knew this was a lie. She wanted to tell him she loved him, that he had been a strength for her and that she would miss him more than she knew how to say, but she could only repeat "Father" once more, before the soldiers were at the door.

Halfway down the front steps, Father Weiss turned. "Some Mozart would be nice, I think. That Sonata in F Major? Perhaps you will open the window, so all can hear."

"The Mozart," Hana said. "Yes." And she rushed to the conservatory and threw the window open wide. Rain blew in, but Hana ignored it, went to the piano and began the sonata. She played it all the way through without once looking out, but she knew when she had finished that the transports had long since gone and that the shiny streets were empty.

Raja came, the following month. It was the middle of the night, and Hana lay, not sleeping, in her bed, when she sensed that someone was there, beside her. Hana knew at once who was there, but, though she longed to reach over and touch her sister, she waited for Raja to speak.

"*Shalom*," Raja said, then laughed. "The Zionists teach us Hebrew."

"My dear, dear sister," Hana said, turning to face Raja, where she lay on Anton's pillow although she could not see her clearly in the darkness. "Why are you here? Is it not dangerous?"

Raja laughed and propped herself up on her elbow. "We live for danger," she said in a voice not her own. "The Zionists teach us that, too. They are *Sabras*, Hana, from Palestine, Jews unlike any Jews we have ever known, strong and fierce and proud and free. They teach us to hide, to outsmart the Germans. They teach us, Hana, to kill."

"Why are you here, Raja? You do not come without a reason."

"No, you are right. I am here because you must leave with me. Now. Tonight."

"And the children?"

"Oh God," Raja said. "The children."

"You did not think—"

"I forgot, Hana. Quiet. Now I am thinking."

"We cannot take the children into the forests."

Raja leaned back onto the pillow. "This is so comfortable," she said. "I had forgotten the feeling of a bed, of a feather pillow."

"Raja—"

"Yes, yes. You are right. The Zionists, though, are smuggling children out. They are sending them to Palestine on ships. I will find out if there is room for Pavel and Heidi."

"But you said now. Tonight."

Raja stretched and yawned. "Tomorrow night. I will come for all of you then." She turned and patted the pillow, then rested her head again. "Oh, for an hour on a pillow," she said.

Hana reached over and touched Raja's hair, cut short by a blunt scissors. "Sleep, Raja. I cannot, and I will wake you whenever you say."

"I cannot stay," Raja said, her voice already slow with sleep. "An hour. No more." And she was at once asleep, something, Hana thought, she must have learned from the Zionists also. Hana watched her for an hour and then reluctantly woke her, and Raja stood, slipped to the window, looked out and then turned back to Hana. "Tomorrow, then," she said. "You and the children. You will be ready, yes?"

"We will be ready," Hana said.

But in the morning the transports came, and Hana, Pavel, and Heidi followed the others to Theresienstadt.

The Czech name of the town was Terezín, and it had been founded as a garrison in the late 18th century by the Emperor Joseph II and named after his mother, the Empress Maria Theresa. Terezín was designed by Italian military engineers, and its twelve ramparts formed, ironically, the shape of a star. At the peak of its occupancy as a ghetto for European Jews, in September 1942, Terezín's 126,000 square yards enclosed 53,000 people, among them Anton and Hana Weiss, their two young children, Pavel and Heidi, and Anton's parents, Petr and Eva.

It was, I thought, a good place to stop thinking about this woman. What did I, a Gentile piano teacher in Los Alamos, know of ghettos, of concentration camps, of the transport of European Jews during World War II? And why should I care?

The Anton I found in Terezín was not the Anton I had married, Hana Weissova's diary reads. I flipped back and forth through the pages, looking for more, but there was no more to find. And so I turned instead to her notes for the symphony, the one with which she'd never been satisfied. "Terezín," it was called, and it was comprised of five distinct yet related themes, which were sometimes interwoven though were more often played separately. Were the themes people? Whom would they be: Hana, Anton, Pavel, Heidi—and the fifth? Perhaps they were not people but scenes or events, or perhaps some were people and others were places.

The most often occurring theme was the piano's, in an

unusual cadence of question, question, answer, question. Played in the E-minor favored by Hebrew songs, the melody had their same haunting quality, a tune that lingered in the mind long after the music had ceased. *"Dodi Li,"* I suddenly realized. Unlike *"Dodi Li,"* though, this theme ended with its cadence incomplete.

The Los Alamos Public Library was sorry; it had no books on Hebrew songs. It occurred to me to drive to the University of New Mexico in Albuquerque, but it was Monday afternoon, and Karen Maisel was due in an hour.

Was Maisel a Jewish name? Would Karen Maisel's mother know something about *"Dodi Li"*? Most difficult of all, could I ask her?

Difficult, yes. But I knew I was going to try.

In traditional music, a piece is organized around a central tone and a dominant chord, which is built on the fifth of the tonic scale. The motion from the dominant to the tonic chord feels as essential as gravity and provides the listener with a strong sense of conclusion.

In the twentieth century, though, composers began experimenting with other kinds of pitch organization. Some compositions are organized around chord relationships other than the dominant-tonic; others use two or more keys at once: polytonality.

Atonality is the total absence of tonality or key, a lack of a basic key to which a phrase can return. Arnold Schoenberg, a pioneer of chromatic composition, went so far as to develop the twelve-tone system, a new technique of pitch organization.

With its lack of resolution, atonality alienates the ear, and compositions based on atonal systems are often incomprehensible, or, at the very least, unpredictable. But think: What is the purpose of music? Stravinsky suggests that its essential aim is "to promote a communion, a union of man with his fellow man and with the Supreme Being."

There is no resting place in atonal music, and yet it is a resting place that the ear desires and seeks. A music that demands the suspension of reason, a movement to a dimension where our usual ways of making sense of things no longer apply, can be more than unsettling; it can be frightening. It is, after all, antithetical to everything we have been taught to believe.

After her lesson, I poured Karen Maisel a glass of milk and set some Chips Ahoy—her favorite—on a plate on the table. Then I asked her what she felt when she played, where she felt the music coming from.

Karen gave me an odd look. "From the piano," she said, looking down. But then she looked up. She took a cookie and examined it, took a bite and regarded me over its crescent edge. "That's not what you mean, is it?"

It would be an exaggeration to say my heart took a little leap, but my breath did catch, if only for a second. "What do *you* think I mean?" I asked her. I took a cookie, too, though I've never cared for them, and took an experimental bite. Sweet sawdust. I got up and put some water on for tea.

Karen had finished her first cookie and picked up a second when I sat down again. "Do you mean how sometimes, when I really know something, it begins to play on its own?" she asked, then immediately looked down.

"That's exactly what I mean!" I cried, perhaps a bit too enthusiastically. Then the doorbell rang and we both looked up as Karen's mother Joyce came in. "Hello hello," she said. "How was the lesson? Finish your cookie, honey, we gotta run." She leaned on the archway between the den and the kitchen, arms folded, purse still hanging from her shoulder.

"Can I ask you something?" I said before my nerve could fail. "Are you Jewish?"

Joyce Maisel's eyes narrowed. "Why are you asking?"

"Oh," I hurried on. "Paul's Jewish, too." There. I'd made an assumption. "I'm just looking for something, a piece of music, Jewish music, and I thought if you were, you could tell me where I might find it."

"Did you ask Paul?"

I smiled and shook my head. "Paul wouldn't know."

Joyce laughed, then came over to the table and sat down. "Physicist, right?" I nodded. "God, what a town. What is it you're looking for?"

"'*Dodi Li*,'" I said, then hummed the beginning notes. Joyce joined in on the second phrase, her voice a flat monotone.

"I haven't heard that in years," she said. "Such a *pretty* tune." She reached for a cookie, frowned at it. "May I?"

"Help yourself," I said. The kettle whistled, and I leaped up, surprised, then made a pot of tea. "Would you like some?" I asked, turning.

Joyce looked at her watch. "A quick cup. I could ask the Rabbi," she said. "About the song."

"There's a *Rabbi* here?"

Joyce laughed again. I liked her laugh. It was

spontaneous, honest. "In Santa Fe. We're not real temple-goers, but we belong. That means we get hit up for the building fund, UJA, et cetera, et cetera. Which entitles me to ask the Rabbi a question from time to time."

"Would you?" I asked. I set the tea pot, two cups, and cream and sugar on a tray and put the tray on the table, then sat down. Joyce took a little cream, no sugar. So did I.

"Mm," she said, taking a sip. "Good. Kind?"

"Oolong," I told her. "My mother liked strong Oriental teas. It must be genetic."

She laughed again. "Or habit." Habit. It had never occurred to me. "Sure," Joyce went on, "I'll ask him. What do you need it for?"

It was my turn to laugh, a rusty sound, I thought, not like Joyce's natural ripple. "It's stuck in my head," I said. "I've got to get it out."

"Yuck. I know the feeling. Except with me it's missing keys, forgotten phone numbers, appointments I'm late for—" She looked at her watch again and stood. "Like now. Come on, kiddo," she said to Karen. "Drink up. Hey—" This was to me again. "Nice talking to you. I'll get you your "*Dodi Li.*'"

"Thank you," I said. "Thank you." But it wasn't just the music I was thanking her for.

After Barbara Stewart died, I was afraid to make a new friend. It had taken a long time for Barbara and me to make a connection, and that had only happened because of Barbara's dog.

The Stewarts lived next door, on the other side of a line of Scotch pines that divided our two properties. Their house was the first in a line of duplexes that marched toward town, house after house of mirrored twins, aluminum-sided, shingle-roofed.

I'd always wanted a dog. I wanted, more specifically, a yellow cocker spaniel, a dog that was featured in the first book I'd ever read by myself, *Buffy Takes a Vacation*. Buffy the cocker spaniel had liquid brown eyes and a perfect coat that lay in waves like the ocean I'd imagined but never seen. Buffy belonged to a girl named Margaret, and understood her perfectly and loved her devotedly and without reservation.

The real dogs I knew were less perfect. A Doberman behind a chainlink fence on the way to school terrorized me; the barks of the Chihuahua in another neighbor's house literally hurt my ears. A wandering gang of mongrels—I was uncertain if they were wild or tame—sometimes came and sniffed the hem of my skirt while I convinced myself I was a statue so I could stand very still. I'd never petted a dog, or known anyone who owned a pettable dog. The dogs in my life and the dog in my imagination might as well have been different species, they were so unalike.

Then, one Sunday afternoon toward the end of sixth grade, I looked out my bedroom window and saw Barbara Stewart playing with a cocker spaniel puppy in her yard. It was black, not blonde, but I knew a cocker spaniel when I saw one, and I opened my window so I could listen as well as watch.

"Here, Tony," Barbara said, and the puppy raced to her and licked her face. "Good dog," Barbara said, then threw something. "Go get the ball." The puppy ran off. Then the scene repeated itself. I watched. I listened. And then I gathered myself up, went outside, pushed through the Scotch pine, and made friends with Barbara Stewart. And with her dog, Tony.

Six years later, and two years after my mother, Barbara Stewart was dead. Barbara's parents gave Tony, whom they couldn't bear to have around, to a family in Española. I wished they'd asked me. But I soon went off to Rochester, where my studies demanded enough time that a dog didn't seem a possibility. Nor did friendship, though I watched others flourish around me. I watched, and I listened, and I wondered at how easily it was done. Easy for others, I should say.

My mother had taught me without ever saying a word that one shouldn't burden another with one's troubles. All around me, girls whined about boys, and other girls commiserated or laughed or stole the boys away. But it wasn't something I could do. Sometimes, in my bed late at night, I'd have conversations in my head with Barbara Stewart, conversations unlike any we'd ever really had. Barbara would explain the way friendship worked, the things that mattered to other girls, and why those things didn't matter to her or me.

Then I would realize that Barbara was dead, so that, of course, those things no longer mattered to her. But I had no such excuse. I was different, and I could feel that difference so acutely that at times it had an almost physical pain, a sharpness that jabbed and then twisted. I sometimes wondered if a heart, when broken, could hurt that way, could jab and twist. What a foolish girl I was.

They were all there, at Terezín: the strings, the woodwinds, the horns, the percussion. And they were all playing in an open square as the line of transports Hana, Pavel, and Heidi were a part of pulled into the camp. Even old Werner Friedman, who'd retired from conducting the year before, was there, his baton etching the rhythms a moment before they were played.

There were cobbled streets and stone buildings, two and three stories high. Everywhere, people were working: hammering at the rising frames of buildings; carrying stones and bricks from one place to another. A group of children sat before the orchestra, striking makeshift drums and tambourines in time. Overhead, the sky was a brilliant June blue.

This is not so bad, Hana thought, a child tucked snugly under each of her arms. At a large stone outdoor oven, she saw loaves of bread being shoveled in by a man she recognized as Mr. Beltok, the baker. Under a grove of fruit trees, two old men pondered a chessboard set on an upturned wooden crate.

The orchestra was playing Beethoven's Ninth, and now it moved into the final movement, the Ode to Joy. The children rose and set down their instruments, filed into two rows in front of Mr. Friedman, and, at his cue, their perfect voices rose into the afternoon. Hana was at first surprised to hear this difficult piece being sung by children.

But now their transport abruptly stopped and swarms of soldiers appeared. "*Achtung! Achtung!*" they cried, hurrying everyone off, forming them into tidy rows. Then they began a roll call, interminably long while the sun beat down, and then the lines were directed to pass by a table and chair where a thin-lipped blonde officer sat, with a riding staff pointing each person in one direction or another: men to the far left; women to the far right; children and the elderly to two other groups toward the center.

"Oh God, oh God," a woman next to Hana said over and over, as if the words were themselves a prayer. Men who were not in uniforms appeared with sticks to hurry them along, not Czechs, surely. Heidi began to cry.

Hana leaned toward one of the stick-men. "My husband," she said. "How will I find him?"

The man pushed her back into line with his stick. "Move along. Move along," he said.

"Anton Weiss?" Hana persisted. "Perhaps you know him?"

"No talking!" the man cried, glimpsing quickly over his shoulder to see if any soldiers were watching.

"Mama," Heidi whimpered. "I'm hungry."

"Oh God, oh God," the woman repeated.

"Quiet," Hana hissed at her. "Enough. You are upsetting my children."

The woman turned and gave Hana a look filled with contempt. "Do you not see what they are doing? Culling, gleaning, sorting, deciding." And she turned back around and resumed her chant.

When it was Hana's turn to file past the man, his pale blue eyes moved up and down her body in an almost lazy way. "Name?" he asked.

"Hana Weissova."

"And what do you do, Hana Weissova? We have found the Jews so talented. Tell me, what is your talent?"

"I am a pianist," Hana said.

The man laughed. "How delightful! Fritz!" he called to a young man standing rigidly near the table. "Here is another pianist. Take her to Herr Friedman, and see if *she* can meet his rigorous standards." Fritz stepped forward and grasped her elbow firmly.

"My children—" Hana said.

"Yes, yes," the blue-eyed man said, already looking at the next woman in line. "They will be in the children's barracks."

"Quickly!" Fritz said. "Come! Come!"

"Mama!" Heidi cried from the edge of the group of children. Pavel hovered protectively over her.

"Stay with your brother!" Hana called. "I will see you soon." She tried to watch the children over her shoulder, but Fritz hurried her away.

Surely Werner Friedman recognized her, but he gave no indication that he did. Fritz still held her elbow firmly, and now wore a somewhat frightening smirk.

"What is your background?" Friedman asked, and Hana told him. She'd played with him, with the Prague Symphony, on more than one occasion, but she did not mention it. As she spoke, she began to recognize faces in the orchestra: Marya Novakova behind a cello; Otto Brozan with a clarinet.

"Bring us the piano!" Friedman ordered Fritz, and, to Hana's surprise, the young soldier hurried off. "Hana my dear," Friedman said. "Are you well?" His eyes darted all over while he spoke, always watching, always wary.

"Have you seen my husband?" she asked. "Anton. Is he here?"

"Yes, yes. Anton is here. He is helping to organize the library. A fine library, Hana. Terezín is a place of culture, and of learning." His voice seemed remarkably free of irony.

Across the wide expanse of the square, Hana saw Fritz hurrying two men along. They were pushing a makeshift upright piano set on a dolly, its wheels catching in the grass and clods of dirt. "Fritzel, Fritzel," Friedman said quietly. "You are a fool."

Fritz rushed ahead of the men, came up and saluted smartly, clicking his heels. "Your piano, Herr Friedman," he said with an expansive gesture. Then the piano arrived, the two men who had pushed it breathing heavily.

Friedman turned to Hana. "Perhaps you will play for us, Mrs. Weissova?"

Hana stood before the keyboard, then was given a chair by a violinist. "What would you like to hear?" she asked.

"Our German hosts are very partial to Herr Beethoven," he said. "A sonata, perhaps? The 'Moonlight'?"

Hana nodded and began. The piano was horribly out of tune, and its damper pedal stuck. Still, she played. When she finished the "Moonlight," no one said anything, and so she went on and played the "Pathetique." Fritz stood by woodenly. He had no idea it wasn't all the same piece.

When she stopped, Friedman cleared his throat. "This one will do quite nicely, Fritzel," he said. "But we must do something about the damned piano."

"What is wrong with the piano?" Fritz asked, looking alarmed. He was really quite young, perhaps not even eighteen.

"Fritzel, Fritzel. It needs a piano tuner. Perhaps you could check your lists and find out if there is one here."

Fritz saluted once again, clicked, turned, and was gone. Friedman shook his head after the boy, then turned to Hana. "You must be hungry," he said. "And tired. One of the women will help you find out where you will be." He scanned the violins and a young woman stood up. "Ah, Rita. Good." He turned back to Hana. "We rehearse every morning from 9 o'clock until noon. It makes the mornings pass."

"Will I see my children?"

"This is not a prison, my dear. Yes, you will see your children." Once again his voice was free of irony.

"Come, Hana," said the young woman called Rita. "We will find out where you live."

"*Dodi Li,*" I discovered, could be played in counterpoint to the third movement of Beethoven's Ninth, though I cannot say what led me to my experiment. When Paul got home from work, I was playing the two pieces in a D minor rondo, and the effect was electrifying. Or so I thought.

"What on earth is *that*?" Paul asked, apparently less satisfied with the result than I was. "That sounds like—is it '*Dodi Li*'?—but what's the other part?"

"Do you know '*Dodi Li*'?" I asked him.

"All Jews know '*Dodi Li,*'" he said. "It's piped into our blood."

"What does it mean?"

"I don't know. I don't remember much Hebrew. No, wait. I think it means 'dearly beloved.' I think it's a wedding song. I'm not sure. Why don't you call my mother?"

I already have, I thought but did not say. Paul was in the kitchen. "You want a drink?" he called, as he did every night.

"Sure," I answered, closing the piano and rising to join him. A wedding song. What a curious theme for Hana Weissova to choose.

While some twentieth-century composers were experimenting with the twelve-tone system, others were returning to their roots for new methods of musical expression. One style in particular was pioneered by Bela Bartok, the Hungarian composer born in 1881, who fused folk elements, classical forms, and twentieth-century sounds into his work.

Using old Hungarian and Rumanian folk tunes as a base, Bartok added dissonant accompaniments, creating a music that is unusually expressive. Fast movements may convey a primitive brutality while slow movements may feel bleak or pessimistic. Bartok reintroduced traditional forms such as the rondo, fugue, and sonata, but even while employing dissonance, polychords, and tone clusters, his works were nonetheless organized around a tonal center.

The ultimate effect of a Bartok composition is one of emotional intensity. The listener moves from quiet reflection to unharnessed frenzy to exciting fanfares to disturbing dissonance. A man who himself left Europe in 1940, Bartok was all too familiar with the unmitigated horror of twentieth-century life, a horror that his music all the same manages to transgress.

Bartok's Mikrokosmos is a set of 153 piano pieces for children, ranging from the simple to the technically challenging. Though for most of my students I do not use Bartok at all, but rather the usual progression from Haydn to Bach to the simpler Beethoven sonatas, there is the occasional student who seems she might actually continue playing past the age when her parents are making such decisions. For these, I dust off the Bartok, as much to assess a reaction as to measure talent.

I had begun to hope that Karen Maisel might be such a student, though her playing continued to be unremarkable.

A teacher must sometimes look beyond the immediate evidence to evaluate a student's potential: a future Georgia O'Keeffe limited to pastoral watercolors, or a young Katherine Anne Porter restricted to 1-3-1 essays, might never reveal her real talent within such confines. The alert teacher may notice, though, another quality quite apart from rote reproduction: a gift of observation; a way of seeing, or of listening.

Karen, I believed, missed very little. Even as she played her dutifully memorized exercises with a small part of her being, her eyes darted around the room, lighting on the pattern of the dracaena's leaves, or the weave of the Two Grey Hills rug. In the kitchen, while her mother and I talked, Karen would stare off, seemingly into space, but when I followed her gaze, it would be resting on a band of light across the tiles, or the chipped handle of my mother's white teapot, which I still use. At the sound of a bird outside, or at the sudden hum of the refrigerator, Karen would be quickly attentive, her head atilt. I noted all these things and began, I suppose, to hope.

Joyce had brought me a Xeroxed copy of "*Dodi Li.*" The lyrics were written in phoneticized Hebrew below the notes, but also appeared at the bottom of the page in right-to-left Hebrew letters. There was something ancient and mysterious about those letters, as if they contained far more than mere words, and I touched them with the tip of my forefinger, curious.

"Can you read this?" I asked Joyce, pointing.

"Oh God!" she said, leaning over toward where I pushed the paper between us. "We're talking *slow*. Let's see. '*Doe deh*,' no, '*Doe dee lee*,' well, of course! I could have faked *that*, huh? Does Paul know Hebrew?"

I drew the paper back. "No," I said, though of course I had just discovered he did know a bit. There was so much I didn't know about my husband. But then, there was much he didn't know about me.

"Too bad," Joyce said. She looked over at Karen, who was slowly tracing the bevel of the table with her finger. "Kare? You about ready?"

"I gave Karen a new type of music to try," I said. "Bartok. It's very modern—you may find it disturbing."

Joyce laughed. "Tin ear," she said, pointing. "None of it disturbs me. Come on, kiddo."

At the door, I touched the music Karen clutched to her chest. "I don't just want you to learn it," I said. "I want to know how you *feel* about it."

"Okay," Karen mumbled, ducking under her mother's arm to get out the door.

It is possible that those who experience the deaths of people close to them when they are young feel themselves apart from those who have not. It is not an elitism so much as a protective device, though whether it is self-protective or shielding those others is more difficult to say. *You cannot know*, is what we think of those who murmur well-meaning platitudes. *How lucky you are.*

My mother, and perhaps Barbara as well, was lost to me long before she actually died. My father, though, who died in his sleep when I was thirty, was such a presence that he has continued to occupy my life in much the way he did when he was alive. "Get out," he tells me. "Do things. Make friends. Make a difference."

My response, when I was a girl, was to tell him that I would, when I finished this sonata, which, if it did not satisfy him, at least mollified him. When I was older, and Paul and I were back in Los Alamos and I'd begun to take in piano students, I would say, "I am," and give him examples, both real and invented.

One night, shortly before he died, he came for dinner, and after we'd eaten, he and Paul relaxed in the den, discussing Lab politics. I sat down at the piano, selected a Debussy nocturne, and began to play.

I don't know how long my father had been standing behind me when I became aware of his presence, but when I did, I fumbled, and then stopped. He reached across my shoulder to touch the glossy rosewood above the keys. "Your mother," he said. "And you." He did not elaborate, and it chilled me.

"I wish I had her talent," I said.

"No you don't," he answered at once. Then he stroked the wood again. "It's enough that you have her piano."

I wanted to ask him what he meant, while at the same time I was stung, as if his words had been: *You have no talent.* My father and I spoke easily to each other, but our words had no substance behind them, and never seemed to say what we meant.

On the other hand, while my mother and I had seldom spoken, our mutual silence said much more. Words, in the end, are the most futile form of communication. It is silence that speaks, silence, and music, which has a language all its own.

The three floors of the old building had been converted to dormitories, rows and rows of bunk beds lined against walls. Hana was assigned a lower bunk on the second floor, near a darkened window that still managed a view over the narrow cobbled street below and across to a men's barracks.

The children lived in two new structures, a boys' facility and a girls'. Classes had been organized—they were not permitted but the Commandant pretended to look the other way. Father Weiss, weak and pale and sitting on a straight-backed chair, taught the young boys arithmetic, writing simple problems in charcoal on windowshades that the boys daily washed off again. Mother Weissova led the youngest children, Heidi included, in songs and games, and revealed as well a talent for storytelling.

And Anton worked on the library. It seemed that all the private Jewish collections in Prague had been relocated to Terezín, tens of thousands of books, and the cartons were stacked haphazardly against the walls of one of the old buildings. Anton and his work crew of five young men were currently cataloguing what they had before they began the more daunting task of organizing the books into sections.

The work seemed to have given Anton back some life, and his depression had been replaced by his more familiar precision and care. Anton lived on the floor above the library, and like Hana had a lower bunk by a window. If their windows had been clean, and operable, they could have seen each other across the street.

They hadn't made love since before the occupation, but the very fact that it was forbidden seemed to make it suddenly desirable. Other married couples had discovered remote corners and the best times to meet there, and Hana and

Anton, when they managed to talk, shared their newest information with each other. But there were not many such places, and their ownership and privacy were carefully respected. Hana and Anton soon began searching, individually, for their own place and time.

Hana had already been at Terezín a month. The orchestra, including Hana and the frequently tuned upright, was rehearsing a program of Schubert and Beethoven for an upcoming visit of Nazi higher-ups. When rehearsals ended at noon, all adjourned to the dining hall, men on one side, women on the other; the children ate in another building. Married couples vied for the benches where the men's tables abutted the women's, and this day, Hana and Anton managed to sit back-to-back. They appeared to be talking to their neighbors, who in turn appeared to be talking to them. But their neighbors, Dori and Vasil Stoll, were also husband and wife, and attempting to make similar arrangements.

"I do not know why I did not think of it sooner," Anton said. "The library."

"When I strip the beds in the girls' dorm," Dori said, "it is deserted."

"But there is a guard at the library," said Hana.

"That is in the morning," Vasil said. "That is when I am working on the new building."

"The guards are often outside while we work," said Anton. "It is so stuffy in there. And I have made myself a sort of office, in a closet in the back. I am often alone there."

"Surely you could sneak away," said Dori.

"What time of day is this?" Hana asked.

"I could not sneak," said Vasil. "But Herman might look the other way, if I give him enough cigarettes."

"Both mornings and afternoons," said Anton.

"I am there from nine until nine-thirty every morning," Dori said. "Always alone, though there is a guard at the entrance."

"I rehearse in the mornings," said Hana. "And in the afternoons I am at the laundry."

"Yes," Dori said. She was at the laundry in the afternoon as well. The Germans insisted their sheets be washed daily, and had constructed an enormous facility for that purpose.

"Who is the guard?" Vasil asked.

"Perhaps you could miss a rehearsal," said Anton.

"Oh, it is that Klaus, that silly boy from Berlin who is always singing dance hall songs," Dori said.

"The absence of the piano player is too obvious," said Hana.

"Klaus!" cried Vasil. "He will do anything for a little bribe."

"Well, there are so many at the laundry. That might be easier," said Anton.

A guard walked the path between them, but they kept talking: They were speaking Czech and this one knew only German; he thought they were talking to their neighbors, as it appeared. And now Dori *did* speak to Hana. "When we go outside to hang the sheets. That would be a good time. I could watch for you, or you for me. But you couldn't be long. And we would need to find a good route. There is that large open space to be got around."

Hana nodded, just as the shrill whistle blew, signaling the end of the meal, and all stood to go. Hana and Anton touched hands, furtively, and his touch sent a wave of electricity up her arm. She could not remember the last time he had filled her with such desire, or that he had felt that way about her. She would seek out a route this afternoon, and let him know this evening.

But that afternoon it was Dori who whispered to Hana, "I am going now to look." Each held the end of a sheet, which they lifted to the line and pinned in one smooth practiced motion. Then they carried the heavy basket a little further, picked up another sheet and repeated the process. Dori slipped underneath, not even ruffling the edges.

"Be careful," Hana told her. "And hurry." She tried to keep the same rhythm and motion they had together, but her upper arms soon ached with the effort and she had to slow down. When she chanced a look toward the laundry building, she saw a guard looking back down the row at her. She risked a wave. The guard glanced over his shoulder, then quickly saluted his fingers at her and moved on. Klaus. Thank God.

How long had Dori been gone? Only a few minutes, probably. Only five sheets. Hana was coming to the end of this line. Soon she'd have to turn back, down an empty line, more exposed. She slowed her pace still more. *Hurry, Dori,* she prayed. *Hurry. Hurry.*

At the end of the line, she decided to hang the sheets from the same side, rather than ducking under and facing in the opposite direction. She picked up her pace again, trying to erect a new wall of sheets as quickly as possible. At the far end of the line, she saw Klaus walk by again, barely glancing her way. *Hurry, Dori,* she prayed.

But when the shot rang nearby, she knew. Next came

shouting, from several different directions, and then Klaus, from the end closer to her, grabbing her elbow and telling her to come along, to hurry, the very word she herself had just been repeating, over and over.

Dori was standing in the center of the square, a guard on either side of her. The sun blazed overhead in an almost white sky, and the other laundry workers were gathered together to one side. When Klaus pushed Hana roughly toward the group and then went back for others, Hana let out her breath, so relieved she thought she might wet her pants; she'd been certain Klaus had grabbed her to share Dori's punishment.

But what about Dori? Guilt and fear replaced her relief. Now the men were being gathered in another part of the square. Hana searched for Anton, but instead found Vasil. Dori's husband. She couldn't see his eyes, but imagined his terror nonetheless.

The Commandant rode up on his horse. The residents had grown used to this horse, an elegant black animal that it was clear the Commandant adored. He leaned over without dismounting to speak to a soldier who in turn motioned to others; all ran off toward the children's dormitories. Oh God, no. Not the children.

The Commandant, meanwhile, marched his horse close to the front rows of the men, forcing them into straighter lines. Dust flew up from the horse's hoofs, and some of the men coughed, waved it away with their hands. Hana spotted Anton, sliding carefully away from the front row after the Commandant had passed.

Then the children were coming. The soldiers hurried them along, and their teachers helped as best they could as well. Mother Weissova was carrying a very small child with one arm and clutching the hand of one not much larger with her other. Father Weiss was being helped by a group of his boys, who hovered protectively around him as he took his painstakingly slow steps toward the square.

But at last all arrived, and the Commandant trotted his horse smartly up to Dori, the animal's front hooves stomping so close to her feet she jumped back. The Commandant laughed, an eerie sound in the full but silent square. Then he danced his horse in circles, the sound of his voice rising and waning as he turned.

"This woman left her detail," he said. "And so we must hang her." A collective gasp rose from the crowd. "Carpenters," he went on, addressing Dori's husband's group. "Build a scaffold. Quickly. We are all waiting."

He will not really hang her, Hana thought. He is making a show, to fill us with terror, and he is succeeding. But at the last minute he will grant her dispensation, he will show us that he is really a compassionate man, and we will be grateful to have such a kindly Commandant.

But when the scaffold was built, the Commandant himself rode up and tied a rope just so. And it was the Commandant, still on his horse, who lifted Dori and fit her neck through the noose. Dori appeared to have fainted, a little blessing, Hana thought, if there could be blessings within such horror.

And then Dori was dead. Her body swung from the taut rope at her neck, and her arms hung limp at her sides. There had been no struggle, no pain, no resistance: She had been alive, and now she was not. *And it could have been me*, thought Hana. Such a selfish, terrible thought, but it was true. Hana searched for Anton across the square, but his group had already been dispersed. Then she heard the small children and turned in their direction. They too were leaving, but they were laughing, and talking amongst themselves. They had not understood! Oh God. They had not understood. Hana's legs collapsed beneath her and she fell to her knees, in an attitude of prayer. A moment later two women came to either side of her and quickly helped her away.

My knees, too, felt weak. While Hana had outlined Dori's death in her diary, it was my imagination that had taken me to this uncomfortable place.

I stood shakily and went to the piano, opening once again to the first movement of Hana's symphony, but I did not play. The music was startlingly light and carefree, the unmistakable lilt of "*Dodi Li*" skipping through the entire movement.

I could hear the music in my head. I hadn't yet played the symphony all the way through; I hadn't been ready. But now my fingers moved on their own to the keys and played the first sequence of chords: One-two-three, One-two-three. A waltz. But a dissonant waltz. The piano repeated the first three notes of "*Dodi Li*," over and over again.

I had never felt anything quite like it. And after a page, I stopped. It was quite possibly a masterpiece. But I still, I realized, wasn't ready to play it through.

Someone once suggested that music **Three**
sounds the way emotions feel, that music
reveals the hidden patterns of our inner lives in the same way
that mathematics reveals the outer, physical world.

It is oddly comforting to our late twentieth-century sensibilities that even music, and its effects, may have a scientific
explanation. Both music and mathematics build what have
been called ever grander and more coherent unities out of
abstract details, and aim at formal beauty. But there is a
danger in deconstructing a thing of beauty: the sum, after all,
is greater than its parts. We are tempted to take the clock
apart, to see how it ticks (or glows), but can we then reassem-
ble the pieces back into the clock they once were?

In the sixth century B.C., Pythagoras asserted that music
was "number made audible," while T. S. Eliot, much more
our contemporary, wrote of pattern and movement, and of
movement and desire. A movement, in the language of music,
however, is but one section of a much larger work, sections

that are in fact much longer than entire compositions in the twentieth century.

Pattern is not a musical term. Its primary definition is "a person or thing considered worthy of imitation." But pattern has more than ten other definitions as well, one of which is "an arrangement of form; [a] disposition of parts or elements." If these are the hidden patterns that music brings to light, the implication of "arrangement" is that there is an "arranger," someone, or some*thing*, who "hid" these patterns in the first place.

Music implies a God. Or, at the very least, music implies a communion that transcends our physical bounds. Unlike mathematics, music is a very frightening thing to deconstruct.

Physicists are also mathematicians. Einstein's theory of relativity, $E=MC^2$, is stated in the form of a mathematical equation, and without mathematics an understanding of physics would not be possible.

At the same time, the language of mathematics is not a language many understand, and this barrier makes the theories of physics appear incomprehensible. Some suggest that if we were to get rid of the math, physics would become pure enchantment, that physics would be more easily understood outside its native tongue.

It is curious that both my husband and I are involved in professions capable of enchantment and yet seem to have no common language. I have tried to discuss this with Paul, in fact, but that very lack of a common language makes such an effort meaningless. My husband, for example, does not seem to understand what I mean by "enchantment," while I am not certain why the term "space-time continuum" brings him such joy.

But another difference makes itself apparent here: While I recognize that these two phrases may be saying the same thing in our very different languages, my husband laughs when I mention the idea.

But in fact the theories of physics are not so very far from the theories of music. Physics, for example, suggests that we are not so separate as we sometimes feel, while music attempts to forge a connection that proves this so. On the other hand, physics is the science responsible for creating the bombs that were dropped on Hiroshima and Nagasaki. Even at its most dissonant, music is incapable of such destruction.

Paul insists that his current project at the Lab does not involve implements of mass destruction, but the name of the project, which is all I know about it, does not sound like it has a peaceable goal in mind.

"I'm not working on weapons," Paul says. We're eating breakfast, and he's reading the *Journal*, but I'm asking him questions anyway.

"What are you working on then?" I ask him.

Paul puts the paper down and sighs heavily. "Anna," he says. "You of all people should know I can't discuss it."

"Broadly," I say. "You can tell me broadly."

"A space station," says Paul. "All right?"

"What kind of space station?"

"Anna—"

"Okay, okay." I get up and busy myself making a fresh pot of coffee. But I'm picturing this gigantic metal ball. It's manned by robots, and it's full of weapons we can't even imagine. And my husband, the man with whom I sleep every night, controls all this from his office here in Los Alamos.

Physics, I decide, is nothing like music.

Could this be what killed my mother?

Oh yes, I know it was tuberculosis. And I heard, for years, her wet ratching cough as she tried desperately to bring up the horrid thing inside her. When she gave up, she no longer tried to get rid of it, and I could hear it bubbling and growing within her while she slept.

It was the habit of Einstein to illustrate his difficult theories with what he called thought-experiments. Thought-experiments are hypothetical situations which serve to explain concepts such as relativity, and the space-time continuum. The tale of physicists measuring a suicide's velocity from the gorge bridge, in fact, may be just such an illustration, though its truth would not surprise me.

Freud asserted that psychologically induced illnesses manifest every bit as realistically as physically induced ones. A pain in the neck may be caused by someone who's, well, a pain in the neck. Stomach trouble may mean that something, quite literally, is making one sick to one's stomach.

Tuberculosis is an infection that causes a swelling of the lungs. The lungs in turn secrete a mucous which fills the cavities that should be filled with air. A tubercular person is breathing, instead of air, a viscous liquid.

Why might a person *choose* to breathe liquid rather than air? It is our original embryonic state: that might be one explanation. But another is that the person finds the air somehow poisonous, no longer capable of sustaining life.

My mother was there the day the birds fell from the sky. It is a testament to her hidden strength that she managed to go on breathing that poisoned air for another twenty years.

There are birds in Terezín, and in the morning, they sing. Meadowlarks can carry a tune, and their melodies are conversations, a question and an answer. Robins sing, too, the same song over and over again, and sparrows peep and doves coo, and, before she gets up from her narrow stiff cot, Hana allows herself a moment to believe that such music insists on hope.

The camp is getting crowded. All summer, transports have been arriving from Germany, Austria, and Poland, as well as from throughout Czechoslovakia. Many of the newcomers are elderly; many are children. Few are young and healthy, and the character of the camp undergoes a slow change.

Men and women no longer eat together. The carpenters have completed the facility that now serves as the women's dining hall, but the portions are getting smaller, as if the same amount of food is being stretched to feed twice as many people.

Since Dori's death, Hana and Anton no longer search for a place to meet, though they still furtively touch hands, if their separate tasks bring them near each other. Hana hears that the library project is going well, that the Germans are very pleased with Anton's work, but she does not hear this from Anton. They no longer risk speaking, either.

It is rumored that Hitler will be one of the Germans coming for the concert in early August, a rumor that sends a current of excitement through the camp, as if when the Führer hears the orchestra he will see that Jews are not so terrible as he has thought. This is absurd, of course, but hope, Hana has begun to realize, knows nothing of reality. Reality, on the other hand, seems to depend on hope.

The children, when she catches glimpses of them, look painfully frail. Mother Weissova insists that Heidi, who's now four, is, despite her circumstances, a happy, healthy, inquisitive child. And Pavel, Hana has heard, has shown a remarkable artistic talent; there is actually an obtuse hope among some that a future arrival may be an art teacher.

The day of the concert, one of the small chamber groups sets up at the entrance to play as the visiting dignitaries arrive. Members of the large orchestra are wearing their best black suits or dresses, and are setting up their chairs behind a newly hung pair of curtains at one end of the women's dining hall. Other workers have been assigned to slide tables against walls and set chairs into concert hall-like rows. Orchestra members peek periodically through the curtains to see who is there and report back. It is Marya Novakova who hisses excitedly to Hana: "It's Anton! He's right here, not ten feet away!"

Hana checks quickly for guards and then hurries to the gap. Anton's back is to her, and she watches this back for a moment: it is much more muscular than the one she remembers. Anton's hair has been very recently cut, and his skull shows dark beneath the blonde bristle. Hana runs her hand involuntarily through her own hair; while at Terezín the cutting of hair is not required, one does not style it, and Hana knows without a mirror that hers falls limply around her face.

Anton turns and sees her, stops, and their eyes lock. Anton's eyes seem set more deeply in his face, dark, and Hana knows hers are probably the same. They could speak in whispers and no one but they would hear, but they do not speak. They stare and stare at each other in a moment that is at once an eternity and far too brief, and then Hana hears Fritz's officious voice behind her: "Piano player! *Achtung!* Here is your piano!" Hana allows her eyes to hold Anton's a second longer, and then she turns and lets the curtain drop.

Hitler, of course, is not there. Eichmann is, and a man it is whispered is Himmler. They all look alike, these Germans, starched into their uniforms, small-eyed, thin-lipped. *But we probably look all alike to them,* Hana thinks, dark-eyed, thin-limbed, too afraid to be angry.

They play a Schubert symphony, a piece that Hana has always previously found highly emotional but now seems simply overwrought. The officers and others clap politely at its conclusion, though they seem to have enjoyed the music tremendously. When the applause stops, Otto rises from his held bow and addresses the audience in excellent German: "There will be a ten-minute intermission, and then we will play Herr Beethoven's Ninth Symphony." The officers murmur their approval as they rise to stretch their legs, and the inmates who have been holding the curtains allow them to drop closed.

The children who will be singing the choral portion of the fourth movement are escorted in by two guards. They have not been rehearsing with the orchestra but only with Otto and a vocal coach, who have adapted this complicated material for their younger voices, and their presence generates excitement among the orchestra members. Men and women alike reach out to embrace children they do not know, to touch soft cheeks, freshly-combed hair, small hands, bird-like shoulders. Many weep, though the children stand stoically, accepting this attention as their due but attaching no emotion to it as the adults do.

Hana reaches for the child nearest to her, a homely, small girl who may be five but could be eight or even ten, and pulls her next to her on the bench in an embrace that pricks too much of bone. "What is your name?" she asks the girl in Czech, and, when the child does not respond, she asks again in German, in French, even English.

"She is a Pole," says Otto. Hana looks up and there he is, leaning his hands on the piano, a Bechstein Grand brought by special truck for this evening alone. "What is your name?" Otto asks the girl in Polish.

"Wanda," she answers shyly, directly looking at Hana for the first time. "Wanda Steinberg."

Hana points to herself. "Hana Weissova," she says. Then, in Czech, "I am from Prague."

"Prague," echoes the girl, and then says, "Krakow," pointing to herself. It is something. It may even be enough, all that Hana can hope for anymore. She draws Wanda close, Wanda Steinberg from Krakow, and she murmurs in the child's hair, "*Je t'aime. Je t'aime*," an incantation whose source she cannot identify, while Wanda experimentally touches the keys of the piano, an E, then an F.

The voices of the children rise at dusk, a sound at once perfect and heartbreaking. Much of the oratorio is a capella, and the musicians allow themselves to listen, to be transported, to rise on the music's wings and take flight.

Hana looks unseeing into the audience, the lovely high voices filling her and then lifting her out of herself. Then, all at once, she does see. She sees the Commandant in the front row between two of the visitors, all sitting stiffly, shoulders back, chins high. Hana has not dared to look at the Commandant since Dori died, afraid her face will betray her complicity, that he will read her face and *know*.

But the Commandant cannot see Hana now. The Commandant is crying. Tears spill unimpeded from the corners of his eyes and course down his cheeks; his eyes are riveted on a child, though Hana cannot be sure which.

Hana thinks that this evidence of humanity should make her feel differently about the Commandant, but it does not. *Hypocrite*, she thinks. *Filthy beast*. Then the Commandant suddenly shifts his gaze to her, as if he has heard her thoughts. Hana wants to look away, but something holds her eyes to his. The Commandant nods. And smiles. Hana feels a bile rising in her throat and gags, swallows it back, and then—*oh hypocrite! oh beast!*—returns the smile. The Commandant nods again and turns back to the child. And Hana turns the page and, on her cue, resumes playing.

From November 1941 to July 1943, Theresienstadt was run by a man named Siegfried Seidl. After the war, he was tried and sentenced by a Czechoslovak court, and hanged. I would like to think that Hana Weissova was present at that hanging, but most probably she was not.

Considering it was a concentration camp, Terezín's musical activity was remarkable. Even before a legless piano was discovered in an unused basement, choral groups and chamber orchestras were flourishing. By the end of 1942, a committee of the Jewish Council called the *Frezeitgestaltung*, sanctioned by the SS command, was overseeing the organization of cultural activities and arranging performances of the many orchestras.

Musicians "employed" by the *Frezeitgestaltung* were exempt from regular work duties, a situation that helps to explain the prodigious amount of composition that went on at the camp. At the same time, personnel in the orchestras was in a state of flux: transports "to the East," to Auschwitz and Birkenau, meant positions opened up far too often.

The training and leanings of the composers ranged from traditional to avant-garde to jazz, though the inclusion of folk themes—often cleverly disguised within polytonal structures—was a common thread. Czech songs, Yiddish lullabies, Hebrew prayers, and Israeli work songs all found their way into Terezín compositions, and were often sung by the many talented opera singers interred at the camp, although, as with the musicians, turnover was a given for these performers as well.

Terezín was the SS's "model camp," peopled with the "elite" of European Jewry, though in the Nazi master plan for the extermination of the Jewish race, still only a waystation before transport to Auschwitz. But, unlike at other camps, its day-to-day activities were run by a Jewish Council; its inhabitants had their own clothes; and, provided they could get a sought-after ticket, these same inhabitants could attend the concerts given by their talented fellow Jews.

But while the variety of music played at Terezín reads like a roster of old masters and modern composers, conspicuously absent are the works of Richard Wagner.

Wagner, like Hitler, was a rabid anti-Semite (and, also like Hitler, was rumored to have a Jewish skeleton in his ancestry). And while it was Wagner who is responsible for the musical drama that defines modern opera, it was also Wagner's works that became the inspirational music of the Third Reich.

The musicians of Terezín selected music for its merits, without allowing prejudice due to national origin to color their decisions. But Wagner reminded them of where they were, and why, and reminders were not necessary.

The prelude to Wagner's *Tristan and Isölde* may be one of the most transcendental compositions ever written. The strings spiral upward while the music swells in a crescendo that seems to yearn toward eternity. One of my professors at the Rochester Institute of Music suggested that the creation of such a piece of music was an epitaph few could achieve but to which all should aspire.

This professor did not mention Wagner's politics, and, if asked, he would have said, *Why should I?* There are many artists whose politics should arguably be separated from their art: Ezra Pound comes to mind, as does T. S. Eliot. But do we honor the man or his work? Can the work be honored without giving the man homage as well? With modern writers, like Solzhenitzin and Achebe, whose sensibilities mirror our own, the question becomes a non-issue.

But perhaps it should not. Perhaps art is a subversive vehicle. Perhaps the artist's motives should be coupled with his creation in our assessment of it. On the other hand, artists are only human; perhaps we should forgive them their human foibles.

The short, cold January days kept me indoors, and I pored over Hana Weissova's papers until they showed signs of too much handling, and I placed them carefully into ziplocked bags that I lay inside my piano bench.

I'd found a book about Terezín by a Czech-American musician, a non-Jew who, like myself, had become obsessed with the place and its legacy. I began to wonder whether any of the compositions the author mentioned had been recorded, and decided when the snow and ice had melted off the hill I'd drive down to Santa Fe and see what I could find out.

Which left me with time on my hands. Several times I thought about calling Joyce Maisel and inviting her family to dinner, but my hand always froze on the receiver: What would I say? And planning one night's dinner party would make but a small dent in the yawning space of time that opened before me.

Oh, I played. I played, and I entertained my young students five afternoons a week. I cooked breakfast and dinner for my husband and packed him daily lunches, and I dusted and I vacuumed and I read, haphazardly, as always.

It was something I read that sent me to the attic, reached via a pull-down ladder in the attached garage. It was a recipe, of all things, a recipe for *linzertorte* that I was certain my mother had once made (my mother who so seldom cooked or baked), and I determined to go through her things and find it.

It is not so odd that I'd never opened those boxes before. For years, they sat in a back room at my father's house, and Paul had moved them to our attic when my father died. My father's papers were, of course, the property of the Lab or the Army—I wasn't sure which—but my mother's had been packed away thirty years ago (by whom? I didn't know that, either) and now awaited me: five medium-sized boxes with that dry cardboard smell peculiar to things stored in the southwest, closed with yellowed tape, labeled in black marker by a hand I didn't recognize.

Whoever had done the packing had done it quickly. There was no method of organization to the cartons' contents, and little boxes of costume jewelry (oh, I remembered that butterfly brooch! those silver clip-on earrings shaped like roses!) lay amongst faded invitations, cocktail napkins, yellowing scores of symphonies and sonatas, old unlabeled photographs, abandoned lists of things to do.

I opened one up: a list of things to do, written on the back of a flyer announcing ancient supermarket specials (*iceberg lettuce 19c; homogenized milk 23c*) with a blue fountain pen in my mother's cramped, spidery scrawl. *Dress for Anna*, it said. *"Tsolidschaya" vodka. Leon's blue suit to dry cleaners. Candles for mother's candlesticks. Tangerines. French Suites #5 in G Major.*

I was crying. I hadn't realized it until the tears dripped onto the list and smeared a thirty-year-old "t." Why should I cry over a list? I folded it and took instead a card from an envelope. *For my mother on her birthday*, it said. I didn't recognize this card, all hearts and flowers, not my style, and when I opened it I understood why. My father had signed my name:

I love you, mommy. Anna. The year was 1948, the year I was born.

I wiped my nose on my sleeve and plodded on, though I'd long forgotten my original purpose. In the third or fourth carton I opened, I came on a small deep white box embossed with a white *fleur-de-lis*, and when I opened it unwrapped the tattered doily folded across the top. But what was this? I lifted it out, two beige-brown squares of—wood? cardboard? styrofoam? The texture on the top was slightly different, smoother than the larger, rougher surface. I ran my finger across it and it rasped, like sandpaper. Then I looked down at the open lid.

Katherine Simms & Leon Holtz, it said, that blue fountain pen again, that unmistakable script. *June 12, 1940.* My God. Fifty-five years ago my mother had wrapped and saved two pieces of her wedding cake and put them in this box. And now I had opened it. Across those years, my mother touched me.

I rewrapped the squares carefully and put the little box back, then repacked the rest of the carton and closed it, too. Then I climbed back down the ladder-stairs and pushed them up into their rectangle, the automatic ceiling panel slipping into place without a sound.

Rehearsals for Verdi's *Requiem* began in the Summer of 1943, but not before a heated debate among the members of the *Frezeitgestaltung*. Hana, now in charge of the activities of the many small chamber groups, did not take part in the dispute, though she followed the arguments of the two sides with fascination.

While Prague's Jews had long been assimilated, newcomers to Terezín included Jews from all over eastern and central

Europe, and it was these who raised the most vocal objections to performing what was, after all, a Roman Catholic mass for the dead. Just as vehement were the project's supporters, who argued that the *Requiem* was above all an exquisite opera but that, at the same time, a prayer for the dead—no matter what religion it originated in—was not a project without meaning. Rumors of what happened to those "sent east" had long since filtered back to the camp, and, whether one chose to believe them or not, a prayer was not out of order.

The more secular argument prevailed, and four soloists and their alternates began rehearsals with the accompaniment of a sole pianist, a role Hana shared with the young composer Gideon Klein, who had adapted Verdi's piano-less orchestration into a serviceable one-piano accompaniment, and who played the premiere performance in early September.

Hana sat next to the stage and watched the barracks fill with those fortunate enough to obtain tickets, now as valuable a commodity as cigarettes and loaves of bread. It never occurred to Hana that the importance of cultural activities to Terezín's occupants was extreme; to Europe's *intelligentsia* they *were* as important as food and sleep.

The audience for the premiere was not a surprise: members of the Jewish Council, their families and their closest friends; and relatives and friends of the principal performers. This did not include Hana's family, since she was not playing this night.

When the audience was seated, the performers filed onto the stage and the barracks became silent, the audience watching the soloists expectantly. Hana watched Gideon Klein take advantage of this anticipation, lift his hands above the keyboard and then keep them suspended there for a moment longer than necessary while he made eye contact with each of those in the front row.

Then he dropped his hands to the keyboard and played. Hana felt she could not hope to have the talent of Gideon Klein, decided she would never play again, and then a moment later was overcome with the desire to play at once. She slipped out a back door to the practice room in the next barracks. Her authority as a *Frezeitgestaltung* member was enough that her movement no longer elicited alarm among the guards.

Her initial impulse was to play what she had just heard, but the much-abridged music sounded oddly attenuated without the accompanying oratorio and she switched to a series of Chopin *Etudes*. From across the alley, the *Requiem* occasionally swelled loudly enough to reach the room where Hana played, and then she would stop and strain to hear more clearly, though she could play the entire piece in her head if she wished. In the silence left when she ceased playing, she suddenly heard another sound, a scurrying movement, and looked quickly in its direction to see something scuttle into the shadows at the other end of the room. "Who's there?" she said, her voice startling. When no one answered, she rose and walked toward the shadows. There, huddled behind a chair, clutching a crayon and a treasured piece of paper, cowered her son, Pavel.

"Don't tell," he whispered.

Hana knelt next to him and drew him to her in an embrace he did not return. "Pavel," she said. "I am your mother. Why would I tell? I am so happy to see you! My little love! Are you well?"

"You can't tell," Pavel said into her neck.

"But what are you doing here?" Hana asked. She reached

for the paper the boy clutched tightly and then relinquished, and smoothed it out on the floor next to them: it was a drawing of herself, playing, a quick sketch which nonetheless captured both the movement and the essence of the player. "Oh Pavel," she said. "This is wonderful!"

Pavel squirmed out of her grasp and made to run out, but she grabbed his ankle. "Keep it then," he said, "if it means you won't tell."

"Pavel," Hana said, releasing her hold on his ankle. "I won't tell." But the boy was already gone by the time she said it.

The day after the premiere of the *Requiem*, another transport left for the East. Among those on it were two of the *Requiem*'s soloists, and Pavel Weiss, Hana Weissova's six-year-old son. Hana hoped he knew she had not told.

The *Requiem* proved so popular that performances continued throughout the winter of 1943–1944, and it was one of the pieces selected by the SS for the visit of the International Committee of the Red Cross in late July of 1944. The Nazis had decided to film this event, and so for weeks beforehand, Terezín's inhabitants were enlisted for sprucing-up activities: painting, gardening, brickwork. Even *Frezeitgestaltung* members were not exempt from these work details, but the change in routine generated a lightheartedness the detainees had not felt for some time.

Hana was assigned to work in the garden, as was Mother Weissova, and the two women knelt side-by-side, placing pansies and impatiens at the intervals proscribed by the careful SS planners. Neither mentioned Pavel, though he was foremost in both their thoughts; instead they kept their conversation resolutely free of import. When one of the *Requiem*'s sopranos came and fetched Hana for rehearsal, Hana and her mother-in-law embraced quickly and lightly. "I will see you tomorrow," Mother Weissova said.

But the camp was too crowded to present the ideal image the SS wished to project to the outside world, and the next day a large transport left with Hana's in-laws, her daughter Heidi, and her husband Anton.

Although the SS had requested that Gideon Klein play the piano accompaniment for the special performance, Klein insisted that Hana play. "A requiem is not unlike a *Kaddish*," he pointed out to her.

"They are not dead," Hana said.

"Of course they are not," Klein agreed. "That is all the more reason for you to play." And while Hana did not pretend to understand his logic, she did play. "*Dies irae*," the chorus sang, and, for Hana, it truly was a day of wrath.

While Gideon Klein was sent to Auschwitz in the Fall of 1944, he did not, as so many of his fellow transportees did, die there. He was moved from camp to camp as a worker, until he died in Führstengrabe at the end of January, 1945.

It has been said that all art aspires toward the condition of music. In the twentieth century, this statement has acquired another dimension. Artists, after all, seek to communicate with their audiences, but science insists that it is the material rather than the transcendent that is the guiding force of humanity. Transcendence has been left to those at the fringe of society, a fringe often mocked, or outright feared.

One way modern composers have chosen to address the increased fragmentation of life in the twentieth century is to create a more fragmented music. But while expressionist melodies often seem chaotic, they in reality are almost obsessively concerned with order. For this reason, the ultimate effect of such a piece is not disorientation. Because the order is so mathematically precise, in fact, the careful listener is ultimately impressed with the piece's intensity rather than its seeming lack of structure. And so, although modern compositions such as this are often quite short, their effect is disproportionately large.

It is possible that we have learned from our fragmented lives that big does not necessarily equal effective. It is possible that we have learned to cull our lessons, and perhaps our transcendences, from the small spaces in which they are allotted to us.

I told Paul about the wedding cake. "Why would she do that?" he asked.

"It's what people did," I said. "For luck."

"A lot of good it did her."

"I just keep thinking about her packing it and me opening it, fifty-five years later."

"Why?"

"The connection. I touched what she touched."

Paul laughed. "Anna, you *are* talking about your *mother*. You touched what she touched all the time."

"But fifty-five years—"

He laughed again. "I guess I don't see what you're getting at," he said.

I rose from my seat. "All finished?" I asked. "Coffee?"

"Coffee'd be great," Paul said, looking relieved.

I have my mother's Steinway. I have her Royal Doulton, and her Waterford and Lalique. The antique china cabinet where these smaller things are displayed was my mother's, and her mother's before her.

Every day I see these things, and, particularly the piano, touch them as my mother did. Perhaps Paul was correct in saying I was attaching too much importance to two pieces of petrified wedding cake. But I knew the wedding cake possessed some fragment of my mother in a way that those other things, things she had possessed, did not.

What is the possessed and who is the possessor? Could it not be argued that the more we acquire the more we become a prisoner to that which we own? This wedding cake, though, was not a possession and hence held far more of my mother's essence than all those things that were. Just as, when she played, the music would possess her, her careful saving of these two pieces of cake was something much larger than the cake itself.

But there was no use trying to explain this to Paul. I could barely explain it to myself.

"Tell me how you met Daddy," I'd demand. There were certain stories I knew my mother was willing to tell, if I didn't ask too often, if I asked only for the ones she'd already told.

"It was on a ship," my mother would say, the distance in her eyes telling me she was already back on that deck. "The *Queen Mary*, a huge ocean liner. Everything was made of lovely, polished wood—the rails, the floors, even the walls and ceilings. And every evening after dinner a band played, and people danced and danced until it was nearly morning."

I knew better than to interrupt or even move, though I had so many questions I'd never asked. Where did she sleep? What did they eat? What did they do during the day, which she never mentioned? Where were they coming from? Where were they going?

But my mother's telling of this tale was her own dream and I could not intervene. Every story, it is said, requires teller, tale, and told, and I, of course, was the latter.

"A tall handsome man approached the table where I sat with my mother, and asked me to dance," my mother continued.

"Daddy," I said. I was permitted this interruption.

"Daddy," my mother agreed. "Tall and dark, though not in that Jewish way—"

I had forgotten that part.

"—and oh so handsome. White jacket—it was summer, but not everyone can wear a white jacket, summer or no. It set off his coloring, that white jacket.

"It was the summer of 1939, the last summer Europe would be what it had been. I was nineteen, and he was ten years older, an officer in the Army. Out of uniform, but it *was* an ocean liner, after all.

"And he asked me to dance. 'May I dance with your daughter?' he asked my mother, who smiled and dipped her chin, and then he asked me. It was a waltz, the 'Viennese;' funny to hear it played by a dance band, but they were really quite good. A pianist from Vienna, a Jew, it turned out, running away. It surprised me, when I found out. Your father looked more Jewish than he did.

"He was such a good dancer, your father. I suppose he still is; we never dance anymore. Where would we dance?" Here she laughed, a tight, odd sound I seldom heard.

"And we fell in love and the following June we were married."

"And lived happily ever after," I added.

My mother would suddenly bring me into focus when I said that, then slowly smile. "Yes, Anna," she said. "If you wish to believe in fairy tales, that is what you must say."

"I *do* believe in fairy tales," I said.

"Good," said my mother. "There is so little else."

Here is my father's version:

"How did we meet? Well, I think it was on a ship. I'd been in Germany, studying their technology, surreptitiously, of course. She was a lovely girl, your mother—that nearly black hair against that pale skin. Frail even then, though at that age it was still disguised by her youth.

"She was with her mother, whom she resembled amazingly. It was like seeing what she would look like twenty-five years later, and I liked that, documented evidence of lasting beauty.

"Her mother died, of course, shortly after we were

married. I wish I'd known her father. 'My father would have liked you,' she always said, and I like to think that's so. We were cut from the same cloth, from what I've heard of him.

"She was very clever, and wickedly funny. I'd catch her mimicking me, and then she would laugh so hard I'd have to join in. Everything made her laugh. I'd never met such a perpetually happy person.

"Of course now I understand that only those who can sink to the depths of despair are capable of such a level of happiness. But she truly was happy. And I was happy, too."

If I had been a child when he told me this, I would have asked what made her not happy anymore. But I was an adult, and I knew what had ruined her happiness.

I had.

So many were gone, and yet Hana remained. All through the long winter of 1944–1945, transports left for the East. But transports arrived as well, bringing strange Jews from Slovakia and Hungary, and, in April, emaciated evacuees from other camps, people more dead than alive, carrying diseases that spread to those already in the camp.

Hana did not fall ill.

Rumors of the Red Army's approach began in April as well, though no one believed them until the SS turned the camp over to a Red Cross representative in early May. Of the 140,000 Jews who had passed through Terezín, only 11,000 were there to greet the Soviet Army when it arrived. Hana Weissova was among them.

When the quarantine was lifted, in August, she returned to Prague, to her large, empty stone house. She went to the Relief Agency and registered, listed the names of all her relatives and the last time she had seen them, and then went home again. She found a piano and arranged to have it delivered to her home, and she found a tuner, a Czech who refused to allow her to pay him.

She began her diary, but drew a line through page after page when she found her words did not say what she wished them to. And then, when the Agency began to have information, she started again.

Anton, she wrote, *1915–1944*; *Pavel*, *1937–?*; *Heidi*, *1939–1944*. Then she closed the book and did not open it again until 1946.

Irena and her parents. Mother and Father Weiss. Her friends, her neighbors. The musicians and composers she'd known at Terczín. Why were all dead and Hana alive?

The Relief Agency employed psychiatrists to help with "survivors' guilt," but Hana could not talk to them. First there was a man, a German Jew, who urged her to return to her childhood. "The roots of all guilt are in our childhoods," he said in clipped German. Hana hated him. The next was a woman, the age of Hana's mother, a Czech from the provinces, a Jungian. "What are your dreams?" she asked.

"I don't dream," Hana said.

The woman looked aghast. "We all dream. You are choosing, perhaps, to not recollect yours."

"That is my choice," Hana said.

"You will make yourself ill," said the woman.

"Then I will be ill," Hana said, and did not return.

Viktor Ullman. Juliette Aranyi. Gideon Klein. Carlo Taube.

Anton Weiss. Pavel Weiss. Heidi Weissova.

Zikmund Schul. Egon Ledec. Rafael Schachter. Dori Stoll.

Petr Weiss. Eva Weissova. Anton. Pavel. Heidi. Irena. Mama. Papa. Raja?

Hana would not dream.

And then she moved to America. To New Mexico. In August of 1947, she opened the diary again and wrote, in careful English:

> *Alice has secured me a position with a University in the western United States. I have left Alice's address with the Agency for Raja. The University is in a place called New Mexico, which Alice says is a desert but also mountains, very hot but also very cold. "You will like it," Alice writes, as if she could know such things.*
>
> *Alice likes it. She has met a man, and is planning to marry again. "And perhaps—" she writes, "—children." Children. Pavel. Heidi. "Don't tell," he said. All I have is a drawing—and it is myself.*
>
> *Still, if I touch the crayoned likeness, I touch the end of the crayon that Pavel touched. I touch it again and again— the likeness begins to fade.*
>
> *And what have I of Anton? Of Heidi? Memories which also begin to fade, which begin to play tricks and change or waver. Heidi is blonde curls. Anton is a touch. I am the only*

*thing which keeps them alive, and day by day they slip from
me.*

*"We all dream," that fool of a woman said. How I wish
I could dream. I would step into my dreams and not return.
I would touch Anton's face, Heidi's curls, Pavel's shoulder,
feel their touch upon my arm. I would hear Anton's voice,
the children's laughter, smell their fresh-washed faces, taste
their salty cheeks.*

*Sometimes at night—but I am awake; I am not
dreaming—I will hear Anton say my name, quite plainly,
his usual voice, as if he is in this same room with me. I am
afraid to answer, afraid I will not hear him again, but I know
I must, and I say "Anton" in that same way, the way I always
did.*

*But I do not hear him again after I speak. All I hear is
the silence after the unexpected sound of my own voice, and
the word that I spoke. Anton.*

I knew how voices of the dead can haunt the living, especially
in the night. The voices I heard were always singular, always
saying the things they had always said: my name, or another's;
common things like "Have you eaten?" or "Where are my
shoes?"

My father would say, "You're wasting your time. You've
got better things to do," an endless series of quasi-commands
I had learned to pretend to obey. My mother, though, if I
heard her at all, would say only my name, a word I seldom
heard her speak, in life.

Lately, there was another voice, lightly accented, melodic.
"Anna," this voice said. "Remember." Remember what? I'd
ask the silence. But the silence did not respond.

Music is unique in its ability to exist in two very different states: potential and realized. Potential music, which lies in the unperformed score, is silent, the product of its creator, while realized music is heard, the product of its performer. No other art can be separated in this manner, and so no other art is perceived in the same way.

The best composers understand that a good performance can only enhance their creation by adding that mysterious element "heart." Such a performance entrances its listeners, moving them to a rapture that the composer could only imagine. It follows that a composer who insists on faithful reproduction of what he has written may doom his creation to mediocrity.

Perhaps analogous to this is the paradox that the large fails to move us. The number 6,000,000, for example, is merely a number to us, incomprehensible in its enormity. "*Shoah*," on the other hand, the Hebrew name for the ritual remembering of the Holocaust which introduces us to individual Jews, personalizes the Holocaust, and so touches the heart of its horror. "Heart" is a small thing, made large in its particularity. In the mathematics of persuasion, whether musical or personal, the product is inverse to the mass.

My mother's playing had "heart." The music that poured out of her piano when she played had an essence of its own, a soul, a presence that lingered long after the music ceased. My own playing, as I have said, is resolutely pedestrian, and I am at a loss to engineer the transition from rote reproduction to something grander.

The performer does not hear the music in the same way as an outside listener. The true performer, in fact, feels the music rather than hears it, and this sensual distinction varies from performer to performer. I suspect that the feeling begins when the listening stops, just as a seemingly difficult question can suddenly be answered when one stops thinking about it. But I do not know how to stop listening.

There has always been music in my life. Even as a child I could differentiate Beethoven from Bach, Mozart from Mendelssohn, Dvorak from Debussy. By the time I was ten I knew I preferred Liszt to Schubert, classical to modern, consonance to dissonance.

These were my mother's preferences as well.

I do not think I am an unhappy person, though I also know I am not a particularly happy one. I do not, like so many these days, assign the blame for any present difficulties to the acts of others in a distant past. My parents, I think, did the best they could, considering who they were, and where they were both in space and time. I was by nature a solitary child, and so the continued solitude of my adulthood cannot be blamed on them.

And yet, as I read Hana Weissova's diaries, I discovered in myself an anger I had not known existed, a roiling, undirected fury, an emotion with which I had no experience in dealing. I never knew what would set it off: a news report from Sarajevo; a driver cutting his car in front of mine without warning; a morning sky devoid of blue.

Where depression is turned inward, anger, I discovered, is turned outward. Depression self-examines, and finds that self wanting; anger screams at the fates and finds them to be at fault. I did not immediately make the connection between Hana Weissova's diaries and my newfound anger, but when I did, I of course began to wonder what it was in them that had tapped it. Hana herself did not express anger. Nor did she point fingers or assign blame.

And perhaps that was just it, that *her* passivity had shoved mine aside. I was angry about the fate of Hana's loved ones, and I was angrier still that she was not angry. I did not want her to react as I would have; I wanted her to be better than I, stronger. I wanted Hana's life to be all mine never would be, and I wanted it vicariously, without any risk on my part.

But Hana had already lived her life, and would not bend to my wishes. She was human, the same as I, and I was human, the same as she. Perhaps it was time for me to stop seeking vicarious experiences and get on with my own life.

By February, the highways were dry and the sun had returned, as it often does in that month. I drove down to Santa Fe one Monday morning, and went immediately to my favorite music store on Cerrillos with the hope of discovering recordings of some of the Terezín compositions.

The long-haired young men at the store knew me, of course. One wanted to know if a tuner he'd recommended the previous fall had worked out; another was anxious to show me the new CD listening stations they'd installed over the winter. It was he I asked about Terezín recordings, drawing a blank look in response.

"You have heard of the concentration camps?" I asked him, not at all certain he had.

"Yeah, sure," he said, "but *music?*" I explained what Terezín had been like, its preponderance of composers. I told him it was possible recordings had been made of their work. "Well, let's check on-line," he said. I didn't know what he meant, but I agreed.

It turned out to mean a computer listing, and my young man (Manuel, with the black ponytail and one gold hoop earring) showed me what he found on the screen. Apparently the computer could pick up cross-references, so that merely typing "Terezín" revealed a CD containing work by Viktor Ullman, Fritz Krasa, Ervin Schulhoff, and Gideon Klein. "This is by a chamber group out of Denver," Manuel pointed out. "Do you know them?"

Denver. It was so close.

"No," I told Manuel. "But I'm thinking of starting a similar group here." As soon as I said it, I knew it was so.

"Oh, be sure to check the board," he said. "You want me to order this CD for you?"

"Yes, please," I said, and, "The board?"

Manuel pointed me to a corkboard I'd never noticed on a back wall, tacked full of cards, notices, and various slips of paper. I read the abbreviations on some with no inkling of their meaning ("*Base* player for NWUF band." "HM jammer looking for gig. No drips." "Progressive salsa bluegrass band needs female LV. No drugs.") Jammer? Salsa bluegrass?

"New Wave Urban Funk," Manuel deciphered when I asked. "Heavy metal. Lead vocalist."

"There's not much classical," I said.

Manuel lifted various papers to read what was beneath them. "You gotta poke around some," he said. "But here— 'String ensemble looking for pianist for quintet offerings.

Classical training preferred.' Gee, it's pretty old. I better take it down."

"Here," I said. "I'll take it." I tried to conceal my excitement.

"You want to put one up?" Manuel asked.

"No," I said. "I think I'll try this one first."

"Up to you," he said with a shrug. I gave him my phone number so he could call when my CD came in, and then I drove down to the Plaza and treated myself to lunch at La Fonda. While I waited for my salad, a memory I had not known I had returned.

"Ladies," my mother told me, "never put their elbows on the table." I slid mine off. "Fold your hands in your lap. When the waiter comes, address him as 'Sir.' Do you know what you would like to order?"

The restaurant at La Fonda was more enchanting than intimidating, despite my mother's sudden penchant for rules. Set in the hotel's enclosed courtyard, its roof rose three stories overhead, and railed balconies circled the second and third floors. Minute motes of dust floated in the muted noonday sun; bright paper *piñatas* hung near the double doors beneath the entrance that led to the Plaza.

Waiters and waitresses dressed in the white cotton and primary colors of old Mexico balanced huge round silver trays of food on one upheld hand. My mother's margarita, which she let me try, tasted bitter, but sported a matching lime green paper umbrella that enchanted me. Mexican music filtered tinnily from invisible speakers, and I was certain that somewhere people were dancing, though I couldn't see them. I had a sudden thought.

"Is this what an ocean liner is like?" I asked my mother.

She turned her distracted eyes to me then looked away again, over my shoulder this time. "An ocean liner? Heavens, no. Put your napkin in your lap. That's right, smooth it. Don't fiddle with it."

Why were my mother and I having lunch in Santa Fe? How old was I? How had we gotten there? (My mother disliked driving.)

My memory decides to answer one of these questions. Here comes a man, a man so unlike my father that he seems another species: he is reed-thin, blonde; his gestures remind me of birds, flying. The man comes up to our table, and says, "Katherine! What a delightful surprise," then kisses my mother on each cheek. He turns to me. "You must be Anna," he says. His voice is funny, not the way a man's voice should be.

"Say 'how-do-you-do,' Anna," says my mother.

"Hullo," I mutter.

The man has already pulled back an empty chair. "May I?" he asks.

"Of course," says my mother, whose eyes look different. "Anna," she says, "this is Carl Mayer. Carl is a violinist. A virtuoso."

The man Carl laughs. "Flattery will get you everywhere, Katherine," he says, scooping up her hand and holding it between his own. "How *are* you, darling? Are you well? Are you *playing*? Please tell me you are."

"I live in Los Alamos," my mother says, as if that is an answer to all his questions. And apparently it is, because Carl laughs again.

"Enough said," he says.

"But you, what are you doing in Santa Fe?" my mother asks.

"They're starting an opera here," Carl says, "and the fools have asked me to organize an orchestra. Me. Can you imagine?"

But now I remember seeing the *New Mexican* opened to an article about just such an opera, about the young bachelor who's been hired as its musical director, how he lunches every day at precisely noon at La Fonda. I'm old enough to read, apparently, and I'm old enough to realize that my mother has employed me in some sort of deceit, or that she is for some reason attempting to deceive me.

"My father is in charge of Los Alamos," I blurt out, though I'm not certain why.

Carl takes my hand and squeezes it. "What a wonderful child, Katherine," he says. "She's absolutely delightful."

But why deceive anyone? Carl Mayer was obviously homosexual; my mother did not make her clandestine plans to begin an affair. Still, she did not want my father to know that she had planned to meet Carl, and she used me as her cover. I could say we met a man that Mommy knew, and it would all seem like a coincidence.

But had Carl been expecting to see my mother, or had she kept her plans from him as well? What *were* my mother's plans?

And here I sat at La Fonda thirty years later, looking around the room as if I expected Carl Mayer to suddenly appear once again, unaged, unchanged, a man, I realized, who had been my mother's friend.

How could I have forgotten someone so important to my mother? Other meetings with Carl tumbled forth all at once: outings to the Symphony in Albuquerque; picnics in the Sangre de Cristos north of Santa Fe. With Carl, my mother laughed and said clever things. With Carl, the things that had attracted my father were once again in evidence.

But I had forgotten. Until this moment, I had forgotten. Why? And what else was there I couldn't—or wouldn't—remember?

When my mother died, Carl Mayer had disappeared, I thought as my waitress brought my salad. "Is there a phone book I could see?" I asked her. She gave me a curious look, then indicated the pay phones up the stairs by the rest rooms.

Perhaps Carl Mayer was still in Santa Fe, and, if he were, he might be able to answer many questions, questions that I hadn't, until I remembered him, even known I had.

September 1947

The little airport building is made of adobe, and sits at the edge of a mesa next to the runway. Alice is waiting for me outside the building with a man she introduces as "Her-bee, Her-bee Stone." Her-bee takes my hand and pumps it up and down in that hard American way and says, as if it is one word, "So waddaya think?"

What do I think? I think, where are the trees? I think, why does it burn my throat to breathe? I think, why does my heart beat so quickly? I think, what kind of name is Her-bee, Her-bee Stone?

Herbie (which is the correct way to spell this name) is "in real estate." Before we get into his car, a black Chrysler with dark maroon seats, he takes my elbow with one hand and waves the other to embrace all the empty space in the valley below us. "Lookit this place," he says. "It's a dream just waiting to come true."

This is the way Americans talk. It is a land without a past, a people who look only forward, to the future. Americans are always making plans, drawing up plans, finalizing plans, implementing plans. One does not hear an American say what happened last week but rather what will happen in the next, as if it is already true.

Americans are direct. They are blunt, but they are also happy people, eager to laugh at jokes which make puns of words or fun of nationalities or races, including, it seems, one's own: Herbie asks me if I've heard "the one about the rabbi, the minister, and the priest," and Herbie, Alice has told me, is Jewish.

As a matter of fact, I have heard the one about the rabbi, the minister, and the priest. I have heard it first from a man who sat with other men at a table behind me in a restaurant at Idylwild Airport, and I heard it again from the man who sat next to me from Kansas City to Albuquerque. I did not understand it either time, though at least the second time, I knew when to laugh.

"Hana's probably tired," Alice says, a phrase which apparently alerts Herbie not to tell me this one. Alice slides into the center of the wide front seat and pats the upholstery next to her, a signal that I should sit there, I assume. I feel as if I must have dreamed Prague, its narrow cobbled streets, stone buildings, gardens and trees. I must have dreamed those mountains and rivers, too, because the mountains here are so unlike them they should be called by another name, and *this river—the Rio Grande, Alice tells me—is flat and sandy and shallow; I do not even realize we are on a bridge over it until Alice points to the trickle of water below.*

Then we turn around and come back; this bridge crossing was for my benefit, a sort of tour, apparently. We drive back up the street we have come down, a street lined on either side with motorhotels and gasoline stations and little restaurants called coffee shoppes, and then we cross some railroad tracks, climb a hill and turn onto a surprisingly lovely street lined with trees.

Herbie turns the car into a driveway and shuts it off, and we all listen to the engine make some noises. "Dammit," Herbie says. "They were supposed to fix that." I realize the car is not supposed to be making these noises.

I am learning such things very quickly. I mention this to Alice, as she sits on the bed in the tiny room where I will be staying until I "find my own place," and Alice laughs. Alice calls me "Honey" now, as if it were my name, and it is near enough my name that I respond to it. "Honey," she says, "You have no idea." I am unpacking my one suitcase into the small dresser squeezed against the wall. This room is unbelievably tiny; I could not, should I want to, fit even a spinet into it.

"At least your English is good," Alice goes on. "Mine was terrible, when I got here. 'Hello. Thank you. Where is the ladies' room?' Do you know Spanish?"

Americans often change topic for no reason. "A little," I tell her. "Poquito."

"Lots of Mexicans here. And Indians. Cowboys, too. It's the wild west, Honey." This phrasing sounds odd with Alice's Czech accent. As if she has heard my thoughts, Alice suddenly switches to Czech.

"You have not heard from Raja yet?" she asks.

"No," I say. I take a slip out of the drawer and carefully refold it.

Alice lights a Lucky Strike and leans back onto the little headboard. "It's easier to forget, here."

I shake out the slip and start over. "I do not wish to forget," I say.

"I know," Alice says. "That's not what I mean." She takes a long draw of her cigarette and then taps the ash into the ashtray on the little nightstand. "I mean, you can go on, here. You can start your life over. It's a different place."

I finish folding the slip and slide it into place, then close the drawer. Then I laugh. "'Different' does not begin to describe it," I say in English.

Alice laughs, too. "You can say that again, Honey," she says, but I don't.

Carl Mayer is listed in the Santa Fe directory, and I note the address and telephone number. Driving home, I realize he must be in his sixties, perhaps even older.

As I turn off at Pojoaque, I realize something else. Carl Mayer may have known Hana Weissova. The idea is so startling that I have to pull onto the shoulder for a moment. Then I realize something even more startling: It is possible that my mother knew her as well. As soon as I think this, I know it is so, and an image flutters somewhere at the edge of my vision: my mother, and Hana Weissova, looking for all the world like sisters, or even twins. They are holding hands, and one points at something and they both laugh.

"No," I say. I say it out loud, startling myself, then check my side mirror and carefully ease back onto the highway. I am letting my imagination get the better of me, wishing for things that have never been.

But why, I wonder, did Hana leave me her papers? Is it possible that these are not mere dreams after all?

MYTHOLOGY tells us that musicians were once afforded special status. A plaintive song could cause a death sentence to be commuted, even elevate its singer to immortality. According to Greek legend, the earliest musicians were the gods, with Athena inventing the flute and Hermes the lyre. Further, when the Muses sang, their voices were so lovely that they moved their listeners to tears, while Orpheus, a Muse's son, could move not just listeners but mountains and rivers as well.

The Bible, too, extols its musicians: David's Psalms, Solomon's Song. Biblical composers praised earthly beauty as well as God's glory, recognizing that what is seemingly simple is deceptively so.

The wedding of music to technology has changed all this; post-modern melodies are no longer meant to please or soothe but instead to show a composer's technical virtuosity. An instrument's natural tonality is abandoned in favor of demanding new or unusual sounds: The strings of a piano may be struck with a broom handle, or, worse, the lid of the piano may be slammed to force a dissonant, atonal roar.

Music, in its earliest definition, meant "the art of the Muses," and more recently, "a rhythmic sequence of pleasing sounds." The advent of science and technology has demanded that we redefine many things: the existence of a Supreme Being; the possibility of extraterrestrial life; the ability of man to design a weapon capable of precipitating his own mass destruction.

But there are areas science has been unable to define: love, and dreams, and life, and death. Music also resists scientific explanation; by its very nature, it cannot be easily reduced to mere words. Still, music can create beauty in the ugliest of circumstances, and it is singular in its ability to help humans transcend, if only momentarily, their mortality.

Memory chooses what it wishes to keep and the rest disappears, as if it never existed. I had forgotten Carl Mayer just as I had forgotten the name of Paul's roommate at Cornell, and, though the reasons may have been very different, the result was the same: When I tried to glimpse into my past I saw broad expanses of emptiness, years that had left no trails by which to trace them.

But now, I had remembered Carl Mayer, and I had his phone number safely tucked in my purse. I put off calling him; what would I say? Then Manuel called from the music store to say my CD had arrived, and I drove back down to Santa Fe with Carl's address in my purse.

The streets around the plaza are narrow and crooked, and

the old adobe walls that surround the houses abut the sidewalks or sometimes usurp them. Carl Mayer's address near the Acequia Madre was marked in tile next to an old wood *puerto* in just such a wall. As is usual in Santa Fe, there was no parking place nearby.

I drove down an unpaved alley to the lot behind a former bookstore and parked in the shade of a cottonwood, then walked back up the alley and around to the street. The sky was a deep blue, but the wind blew with its unmistakable March insistence, moving last year's leaves, ancient dust, and this year's bits of paper to new locations as if that were its purpose. At the *puerto*, I searched for a bell or knocker, but, finding none, I lifted the heavy iron latch and entered the courtyard, then closed the door behind me.

The wind did not enter the courtyard with me, and the stillness made me aware of my stinging ears. I shook my head, then followed the short brick path through now-brown sage and chamisa to a small covered entrance; *ristras* hung from the rafters on either side. Again, there was no bell, but an iron-faced lion on the door sported a ring through its nose. I lifted it and let it drop, then listened for movement beyond the door.

It was very still.

I knocked again with the iron ring, and this time I heard a scraping sound inside: a door opening, perhaps, or a shoe against tile. Then I heard high-pitched barking, the kind that only a very small dog can make, and the unmistakable voice of Carl Mayer, saying, "Oh, be quiet, Sabrina. Honestly." Then the door creaked open.

He didn't seem to recognize me, but I knew him at once; he was remarkably unchanged. "Yes?" he said, wearing an amused half-smile, an oxford-cloth shirt tucked into chinos, a sweater draped casually across his shoulders. He was still thin, still blonde, and still had that air of condescension I'd forgotten.

"Anna Kramer," I said. "Holtz. Anna Holtz."

The half-smile broke into a huge grin, and I found myself wrapped in Carl Mayer's arms. "At last!" he cried, dramatic as ever. "Come in! Come in!" And, with a sweep of his arm, I was in, led to a surprisingly large central room with a skylight and a warm woodstove, parked on an old maroon sofa with yellowed antimacassars on its arms, offered tea, and then left alone for a moment to take in my surroundings while Sabrina, a long-haired dachshund, thoroughly inspected my shoes.

Built-in bookcases. A Steinway, with a Stradivarius left casually on its bench. Oriental rugs. African masks. Overgrown ferns and schefflera. African violets. A shelf of photographs over the piano.

I got up to look at the photographs more closely. Here were Carl and my mother, talking with someone at a party—was it Stravinsky? It was. Here was my mother again, caught off guard in a snapshot in someone's back yard, her hair half-hidden under a wide white band, her eyes obscured behind owl-rimmed dark glasses. The smile she had presented the photographer was not one I often saw, but the face was. This was my mother at forty, when I was twelve years old.

"You have her eyes," Carl said behind me. He'd set a tray on the low table by the sofa and had sat down to pour tea. "No sugar, a little cream," he said, and I nodded. "It's Oolong. Everything's accessible, these days. The challenge of finding the unusual has disappeared, along with many other fine arts." He patted the sofa next to him. "Come. Sit. We have years of catching up."

I obeyed and accepted the cup he offered me. "You don't seem surprised to see me," I said.

He shook his head. "I'm only surprised you took so long."

"I just remembered you," I admitted.

"That's rather odd," Carl said. He paused, took a sip of tea, and set his cup down before continuing. "We were very good friends, you and I."

"When?" I asked.

Now he put a finger to his chin and considered. "From 1958—or was it 59?—until 1965, when poor Katherine died." He looked at me for confirmation. "Good God. You really *don't* remember, do you?" I shook my head.

"I'm afraid your father didn't approve of me," he said, "though that would hardly explain obliterating me from your memory. Not that he's not capable of it."

"He's dead," I said.

"So he is," Carl agreed. "But a *commanding* man nonetheless, wouldn't you agree?" I didn't respond, watched Carl take another careful sip of the still-hot tea.

"Leon and I had no common place to begin a conversation," he said. "Except for your mother, we had nothing in common at all, and as I said, Leon did not approve of our friendship."

"Was he jealous?"

Carl laughed. "Jealous? General Holtz? Hardly. It's just that he couldn't abide fairies. Don't look so startled, Anna dear. I *am* a fairy. I'm afraid it made Leon more than a trifle uncomfortable."

"I don't remember you," I said. "Why don't I remember you?"

Carl set down his teacup and took my hand between his

own. Feeling it, I remembered the gesture. I remembered him taking my mother's hand the same way, at that table at La Fonda. "Poor, poor Anna," he said. "You were such a malleable child. So eager for your father's attention. Your mother's, too, and poor Katherine didn't have a clue as to how to show you she loved you. After she died, I came and packed away her things. Your father stayed in his study, only came out to point where I should set them. 'There,' he said. 'There.' As if by closing that door he was denying their existence. And then he saw me out and I knew I'd never be back."

"Where was I?"

Carl thought about this. "I don't know, Anna. You weren't *there*. Perhaps the housekeeper had taken you to her house?" He shook his head. "I'm sorry. I don't know."

"I'm trying to remember my mother," I said.

"Poor Anna," he said again, then smiled. "You *will* stay to lunch, won't you? I've got black bean soup simmering, and the makings for *quesadillas*."

"I'd like that," I said. I was twelve years old again, grateful to Carl for the direction he was willing to give.

June 1950

    Now that Alice is expecting, I have found a little house of my own, or rather, Herbie found it, a two-bedroom stucco on Amherst just a little ways off Central, close enough that I can walk to the University for classes and rehearsals.

    Although I have purchased a car, a rather nice green Plymouth which seems to float along the highways. This is what I do, most weekends: float along the highways in my Plymouth. I have floated to a number of Indian pueblos:

Acoma, Jemez, Santo Domingo, Santa Clara, and I have begun to learn about their pottery; and I have floated to Santa Fe, and on to Taos, and explored their little back streets.

I have floated along rutted dirt roads through the mountains: the Sandias, the Manzanos, the Sangre de Cristos (the Watermelons, the Apple Trees, the Blood of Christs). I have driven through the Jemez Mountains to the Anasazi cliff dwellings at Bandelier, and continued on to Los Alamos, the birthplace of the Atomic Bomb.

The radio in my Plymouth plays American showtunes: "Oklahoma," "You'll Never Walk Alone." *I practice my English by singing along with them; alone in the car I can sing quite loudly, and have found that the upholstery offers a pleasing resonance. I like, as well, the mournful sound of American blues, and in particular the voice of Billie Holiday, whose voice bares emotions as if they were merely hidden sounds. I envy Miss Billie Holiday her ability to, as the Americans say, "wear her heart on her sleeve," though I prefer my own heart tucked away where I will not come upon it.*

"You should go out!" Alice cries. Alice "fixes me up" with young men she has met at the Synagogue; Herbie fixes me up with the sons of business associates. They all wish to know what Terezín was like. They wonder why I do not have a number tattooed on my arm. What do I think of the Nuremberg Trials? Do I think Hitler is still alive, and living in South America?

But how could I explain Terezín to an American, to these young men who have never seen their own familiar country turned into a nightmare place one hopes she is only dreaming? If I tell them why at Terezín we were not tattooed, they think it was somehow "not so bad."

They do not ask about my children. Perhaps Alice and
Herbie coach them beforehand.

When they ask me about the trials, or that question
about Hitler, I tell them I am an American now. I tell them
that Americans do not look back but only forward, that
Americans prefer the concrete to the imagined: I'm from
Missouri, *I say.* Show me.

This makes them laugh, which is precisely my intention.
Then I can move the conversation on to other things: Have
you ever been to Missouri? *I will ask them.* What is it
like? Have you read the books of Mark Twain? It is hard
to believe that just eighty-five years ago the Colored
were still slaves.

The young men drive me home after dinner, or after the
movie. They pull into my driveway and then walk me to my
door, wait while I unlock it. Then I turn to them as I open
it. "Good night," *I say.* "Thank you." *And I go in and close*
the door behind me before their startled mouths can think of
anything to say.

I have discovered a fondness for good aged Scotch whiskey. I
am not, needless to say, a "lush," but late at night just before
I go to bed I like to pour a little Dewars onto some ice from
my Frigidaire and sip it slowly, feeling its heat move down-
ward from mouth to throat to stomach.

The Scotch frees something in me that I am very care-
ful to keep reined, except for these late nights. I will move to
the black Steinway grand that I have purchased "on time,"
and set the glass down and begin to play.

I may start with Liszt, or with Chopin, with their

studies for piano so full of melancholy and remembering. But soon enough my hands move on of their own accord, playing the themes that I have come to realize have names: Anton, Pavel, Heidi. Dori Stoll. Gideon Klein.

Anton's theme is very stolid, very predictable, or at least that is how it begins. A sudden dissonant chord shifts the melody to E-minor, though the original theme is still discernible.

Pavel's and Heidi's themes are several octaves above Anton's, and, while they share a seed of Anton's theme they soon move off in directions of their own, until they quite suddenly end, mid-bar.

For Dori Stoll I have used a variation of an old Hebrew song. This theme is also the thread that ties the whole piece together, so I suppose it represents myself as well. I have been experimenting with an unusual cadence for this theme, but am not altogether satisfied with it as yet.

Still, I have gone so far as to commit each theme to paper. I am seeing ultimately, I think, a symphony within which all of them will be interwoven, until the last theme, my own, is all that is left. I hear this being played by a lone clarinet.

It is very late when I stop playing. My piano sits by a pair of French doors that leads to a little patio, and I often carry what is left of the glass of Scotch out and sit on the little step. The sky here reveals innumerable stars and planets, the occasional meteor falling to earth. There is no one else about, this time of the night, and the city possesses a silence of which one would not think a city capable. Sitting there, beneath that sky, enveloped by that silence, I feel at once small and inconsequential and aware of the fabric of things, how it is all interconnected, woven with a thread so fragile and yet so amazingly strong.

Anton is with me there; they are all with me there, and I with them. Though I would not be so foolish as to tell anyone else this. Especially Alice, my completely American friend.

The distinction between score and performance entered a new phase with the advent of recorded music, and a side benefit of recording technology has been the ability of artists who may be reluctant to appear on stage to nonetheless perform, and to have those performances preserved for posterity. Thus we can listen to Glenn Gould, Wanda Landowska, and other performers whose unique talents would otherwise have been buried with them.

The more music we hear, the more there is available to our consciousness. In a mere hundred years, the recording of music has evolved from its early tinny renditions to the precision sound of the laser disc. Technology now allows us to listen to the sound of an entire symphony in our home or car, the recorded final chord as resonant as the original, the sound precise and clean and true.

At the same time, psychologists have begun to examine the role of music as an avenue to and from the unconscious. Melodies rise, seemingly unbidden, to our consciousness, melodies that may simply show how we are feeling, or may, on a much deeper level, indicate something hidden, of which we are not consciously aware.

There are melodies, too, that refuse to leave us, leitmotifs which, when examined, may well be revealed as our own particular themes. Considering that our emotional experience of a composition is quite different from that of its creator, this ability of music to express us to ourselves is indeed remarkable. Music may well be the missing link between our dreamed lives and our waking ones.

My mother was sometimes given to humming, a soft distracted sound of which she did not seem to be aware. On her good days, it might be Bach, snatches of a Brandenburg concerto, or a Mozart aria, from *The Magic Flute* perhaps. Other days she hummed melancholy tunes, but on her worst days she did not hum at all, and her silence became the melody, dark and without end.

My father, on the other hand, was a whistler. There is something in the very nature of whistling that says its source finds all right with his world. He whistles snatches of popular tunes, and the listener finds herself supplying the words. *When You Wish Upon A Star. He's Got High Hopes.*

According to my father's biographers, the primary factors in choosing the first atomic bomb targets were that they should convince the Japanese that they could no longer fight the war, and that they be military targets. What is not addressed is that the four targets finally selected were in areas of dense civilian population.

My father has been quoted as saying that the bombing of a metropolis "would serve to illustrate the bomb's effects," though his thoughts on the specific illustration Hiroshima provided are not recorded. Here, however, are the statistics: Sixty percent of the city was destroyed, including an area of total devastation around ground zero of 1.7 square miles. Casualties were estimated at 71,000 dead or missing and 68,000 injured. Did this "illustration" show my father what he wished to see? I wonder. Were these specifics the effects he had expected, for which he had hoped?

And how is it that the man responsible for these statistics could, throughout his life, continue to be a whistler? How is that he could whistle "You Are My Sunshine" without apparent irony; "I've Got You Under My Skin" without a twinge of remorse?

And why should I in turn feel responsible for his decisions, decisions that he after all made years before I was born? Why, unlike my father, am I haunted by images of thousands of mouths forming surprised O's in the millisecond before they are reduced to ash, by echoes of screams that never had the time to erupt? There is no music to accompany this horror, and yet my father was a whistler. To my father's mind, these bombs ended a war, and that's all there is to that.

With the onset of soccer season, Karen Maisel quit her piano lessons. Joyce apparently had told her that it was her choice to make, but that she would have to be the one to call me. I had asked Karen several times for her reaction to the Schoenberg, but was always met with a non-committal, "It's okay." Now, on the phone, knowing I'd already lost her, I grew bold.

"You were intrigued by the Schoenberg, weren't you?" I said.

"I guess," said Karen.

I pushed on. "Which proves you have a talent you shouldn't squander."

"I'm just quitting, okay, Mrs. Kramer?" The beginning of a whine had crept into her voice. "If you wanna think I'm a quitter, fine. But I'm quitting."

"Well, if you change your mind, I'll be here," I said.

"Okay," she said. "Bye." Karen hung up before I could press on further, opening up much more than my 3:30 Monday slot.

I looked at the phone still in my hand, then before I could change my mind, called the number of the chamber group I'd picked up the month before. A woman answered; I heard Schubert playing in the background.

I told her I'd seen her ad at the music store, and that I was a classical pianist.

"Who are you?"

I told her my name was Anna Holtz, and added an explanation that I'd been out of circulation for quite some time.

"You're not any relation to Katherine Holtz!"

I realized then that I had given my maiden name, but decided not to correct myself. "She was my mother," I said.

"God," said the woman. "I heard a pirate recording of her playing with the Opera. Carl Mayer had coaxed her out of her retirement and she just played that one time. She was incredible. And what a beautiful woman!"

"Yes," I agreed. "She was."

"I never knew she had a daughter," the woman went on. "Of course, why should I? But you're a pianist, too. That's so neat. We've got someone rehearsing with us, but to tell you the truth, he's just not *meshing*. The karma's off. Are you free for lunch?"

The woman was so…so *open*. For a moment I regretted calling. "I live in Los Alamos," I said.

"Oh, that's right. Your father was—now I remember."

There was an awkward pause.

"Well, listen," she went on. "We're rehearsing every evening. You tell me what night you can come down and I'll tell Mike—that's the pianist we've got now—that rehearsal's called off."

"That's rather duplicitous," I said.

"*C'est la vie*," she retorted. "I'm Emily Corbett, by the way. Cello. What night?"

Why not? I thought. "Thursday?" Today was a Monday.

"Great! Let me give you directions."

Emily Corbett lived in one of the new pueblo-style townhouse complexes that had sprung up on the southeast side of town off the Old Pecos Trail. She was small, blonde, and in her mid-30s, and wore an embroidered black bolero vest over a white t-shirt and skinny little jeans.

"Oh good, you're early!" she said when she opened the door. "We can get acquainted." She led me into a modern Santa Fe-style living room whose double doors looked across a courtyard to their mirror twin. As we settled into matching southwest-style chairs, a high voice called from the kitchen behind her. "Mom! We're out of Spaghettios!"

"Then make Raviolios, Aaron," she called back without turning her head. "Kids," she said to me, as if I would understand.

"I don't have children," I said.

She glanced at my left hand and noted my wedding ring. "Clever you," she said. "Katherine Holtz's daughter. God, I can't believe it!"

I could change the subject as quickly as she, I thought. "Tell me about your group," I said.

"We call ourselves the Agua Fria Players," Emily said, tucking her legs underneath her. "Paula Thoms and John Engle play the violins, and Louis Sanchez plays the viola. Have you ever heard Louis? He plays with the Symphony, too. We're lucky to have him."

"What are you working on now?" I asked her, trying to keep her from straying onto one of the tangents to which she seemed to constantly veer.

"The Beethoven *Grosse Fugue*? Schubert, no. 14 in D minor, you know, *Death and the Maiden*? And Brahms."

"So why do you need a pianist?" I asked.

Emily laughed. "Good question. You know your music. See, what we're thinking is to do some piano quintets. Some of the sonatas, you know? Schubert's Trout, Opus 114. The Hindemuth—do you know it?"

The doorbell rang and Emily leapt up before I could show off my knowledge, but the others had let themselves in. "Forgot to lock the door again, Em," said a smiling man with thinning blonde hair pulled back into a ponytail. "Boogie man's gonna get you."

The other man, a Hispanic with dark hair cut close to his head, crept behind Emily then jumped up and yelled, "Boo!" Everyone laughed.

"You'll scare Anna away before she even hears us!" Emily protested. Then she made introductions. Nearest to me, Paula Thoms extended a firm handshake.

"The piano's downstairs," Emily told me, already leading. "We practice down there."

On the stairs, Louis Sanchez turned back to me. "Wait

till you hear her play. She's not the flake you think she is."

"What makes you think I think that?"

He smiled. "How could you not?" I liked him at once, something I seldom did.

When I told Carl Mayer about the group, he was delighted. "Tell me who they are!" he cried, and then said, "Yes. . .yes . . .oh, very good . . .yes," when I recited their names. "Will you stay over here with me sometimes when you're rehearsing?" he asked. "It would be like old times."

"I don't remember the 'old times,'" I reminded him.

"Ah yes, the great mystery," Carl said.

Now that I'd "found" him, Carl and I spoke on the phone often, and I tried to visit him a few times a month. He loved to tell me stories about those "old times," and occasionally a small piece would click into place. But nothing more. Yes, he had told me, my mother and Hana Weissova were *dear* friends. Didn't I remember?

Sometimes I could put them into a room in Hana's house, the one I'd seen in Albuquerque. I could seat them on a comfortable sofa, have them face each other, both talking at once, ringless hands gesturing with words, laughter. But I wasn't certain if this was memory or desire.

"Repressed memory's like a lock without a key," Carl said once. "You won't let yourself in. It's you against you." He threw up his hands. "Hopeless."

"But why would I repress it?" I asked.

"There are lots of reasons. Because it's too painful to remember, that's the most common. But I don't think that's it. So maybe because when you did remember it, you were punished."

"I was never punished," I said. I felt my face redden.

Carl held out a palm. "Okay, okay. Sorry. Maybe you thought remembering those things would hurt your father, that if you forgot them, they'd cease to exist."

"He was hardly a man who needed protecting," I observed.

"But he loved your mother," said Carl. "And, in her way, she loved him."

"And we all lived happily ever after."

"I wish you'd consider seeing my therapist," Carl said, not for the first time. "She could help you so much more with these things."

"There's no sense living in the past," I told him. But I knew that was exactly where I had been living.

March 1951

I have heard from Raja!

She is living on a kibbutz *near Lake Tiberias in Israel, our young Jewish State. Until recently, she had been a member of an illegal organization and could not contact me, though she knew I was alive.*

How she had wished to contact me, she wrote. And yet she did not, and for six long years I wondered and hoped and dreaded the words I would finally hear. . .

But now I have heard them, and I am no longer alone in the world. Poor Raja—Josef died in her arms in a Bavarian wood and they buried him there and then hurried on. "It was a quick death," she wrote. "A clean shot through the heart. No pain. I am grateful for that." She did not ask me for details about the others' deaths; perhaps she already knows them.

After the War, she entered Israel—Palestine, then—with the Israelis with whom she'd been throughout the War, and became involved with smuggling in Holocaust survivors.

I am not yet comfortable with that term, Holocaust survivor.

Raja's work meant she had to return to Europe—her command of languages made her especially valuable there. Everywhere, she saw devastation, former cities become rubble-strewn plains. There were few Jews to be found in Germany, where she was sent first, and so she quickly and gratefully moved on to Austria, only to find few Jews left there as well.

The camp survivors seemed to fall into two distinct groups, Raja wrote: those who wished to live, and those who wished to die. The latter stared with vacant eyes, eyes turned inward to view again and again unimaginable horrors from which they had for some reason emerged with their lives. The former, on the other hand, had seemed to close a door on what they had seen and now looked resolutely forward.

Which type was I? Raja asked.

She could not help but believe that since my new address was in America, that I had decided to move forward, which, she added, was exactly what Anton would have wanted me to do. Was it not interesting, she wrote, that we both were somehow stronger in our resolve than our husbands, they should rest in peace, had been? She did not mean to disparage their memories, she hastened to add, but it was clear that we were more capable of adjusting to adverse circumstances, indeed, to any new circumstances. This, she went on, led her to believe that women were genetically stronger than men, a private opinion she dared share with no one but me.

But how did I find New Mexico? She had located it on a map of the United States, and found pictures which led her to believe that it physically resembled Eretz Yisroael. She had seen on the list that Alice Hermannova was here as well—did I see her? Was I playing? Had I remarried? She had not, though she enjoyed a longstanding relationship with a man who had been the commander of her underground group and was now an officer in the Israeli army. Perhaps someday they would marry, though she, for one, was in no hurry to ruin a good relationship.

I had heard, no doubt, that Mama, Papa and Irena never got out of Austria, and were among the first to die at Auschwitz? Horrible, horrible. There are no words to describe it. In Israel, all rise for the daily Mourners' Kaddish; all have committed its ancient words of comfort to memory: Yisgadol v'yiskadosh sh'may rabah.

But even as we mourn, Raja concluded, we must strive to ensure that their deaths will not go unremembered. Did I belong to Hadassah, whose remarkable hospital on Mount Scopus, a place now sadly in Arab hands, reminded all Israelis of what was possible? Did I support the activities of Youth Aliyah and its efforts for orphaned Jewish children the world over? Did I read the American edition of the Jerusalem Post, and see how the desert was being reclaimed for agriculture, how Eretz Yisroael was rising from both its own ashes and the ashes of European Jewry to become a nation of strong and unafraid women and men?

And was I well? Please write to me, Raja wrote, my truest sister among my many sisters. I love you. Je t'aime.

23 March 1951

Dearest Raja,

Such a joy to hear from you, to hear that you are alive, to hear that you are in Israel, our own country, to hear that you are still so much the Raja I remember.

I am very well. I am the principal pianist with the New Mexico Symphony Orchestra, and in addition individually tutor graduate students of piano at the University of New Mexico. I live alone in a lovely adobe house on a tree-lined street only a half-mile from the University, and Alice (along with her American husband Herbie Stone and their son David) lives nearby.

It was Alice who arranged for me to come here. She is with the Economics Department, just as she was at Charles University (remember how she and Anton used to argue while you and I laughed about how little what they were arguing about mattered?), and Herbie sells real estate— homes, land, and ranches—and is very successful. They may soon be moving to a new area called Four Hills. It is miles out from the edge of the city, near the place where the Sandia and Manzano mountains drop to meet in Tijeras Canyon.

It pleases me to think that New Mexico, where I live, resembles Israel, where you live, and yet they are so far apart I wonder how we will ever see each other again. Hadassah, of course, offers tours of Israel, but while my little salaries are more than enough to support me here, they do not allow the luxury of overseas travel.

No, I have not remarried. I feel I am still married to Anton.

Yes, I know about Mama, Papa, and Irena.

I do not agree with you that women are genetically stronger than men, but your vehemence makes me smile: You have not, it seems, changed at all.

Perhaps I have not changed either, though I feel as if I am quite another person, not an older Hana but an entirely different one, separate from the woman who had a husband and children in that lovely old stone house in Praha. *I cannot pinpoint where the one Hana ceases and the new one begins, but can only note that there is nothing that connects them except their name.*

And other names: Pavel. Heidi. Anton.

I do not mean to begrudge you your new love, but for me that does not seem possible. It would seem to profane Anton's memory, or rather, the Anton who is still alive only because I keep him so. Do you remember Anton before the War? How serious he was! And how we loved to tease him! Were we cruel?

This haunts me.

This haunts me, too: The night, just before it all began, when Heidi had the chicken pox. I sat up all night with her, and then Anton came at dawn and insisted I come to bed. I see this night with a vividness that is stronger than mere memory, as if I am living it over and over again. Heidi whimpering in her sleep. Anton tiptoeing into the room. Anton drawing me into his arms.

Enough. My darling Raja. At least we still have each other.

$\mathcal{A}$s a composer whose voice is *five* remarkably distinctive, Beethoven stands nearly without peer, and this is due in no small part to the range of emotion his work conveys. And yet, whenever Beethoven premiered new work, many of his early nineteenth-century listeners found it bizarre.

While humans are decidedly reluctant to accept change, artists must both divine and implement it. It is all too easy to remain in the status quo, to read the same plot over and over again, to paint the same picture, hum the same tune. There is a certain comfort in the familiar, in nothing ever changing, in knowing what comes next.

But to seek such comfort is to fool ourselves, and to avoid living our lives to their fullest. To create is to take a risk, to open a door without knowing what lies on its other side. Our problem with our politicians is that they are *not* risk-takers, but rather risk-weighers who always err on the side of stasis.

Until the mid-1960s, Americans were happily unfamiliar with the politics of complacency. It was the rude awakenings of that decade that led to our now habitual distrust of our leaders. Both Lyndon Johnson and Richard Nixon were masters of a deceit that would cut so deeply their example entered not just the mainstream but the national psyche.

Revisionist historians attempt to ascribe this deceit to events that predate its existence, to the war-time decisions of FDR and Harry Truman, for example. For Truman, the decisions to drop bombs on Hiroshima and Nagasaki were clearly the most difficult of his life, decisions he nonetheless made as a risk-taker who has no political equivalent today.

For my father, however, those decisions were not agonizing at all. But my father was first and foremost a soldier, after all, and his business was war. My father found the second-guessing of revisionist historians bizarre; he was not a man who looked back.

Paul was unable to attend my premiere performance with the Agua Fria Chamber Players, but I wasn't surprised and didn't even—which did surprise me—really care. Carl Mayer came, mingling easily with the other members of my group during the after-concert cocktail party. Louis Sanchez he knew professionally, Paula Thoms he knew from the gay rights alliance, and both Emily and John he knew by reputation.

I worried that Emily's flaky effervescence would put Carl off, so it startled me to find Carl and Emily laughing together exactly where I'd left them fifteen minutes before, though perhaps it was not so much surprise as a touch of jealousy.

"Too bad about Mr. Anna," Carl said as I rejoined them. He turned back to Emily. "Mr. Anna's a very busy man," he explained.

Emily giggled. "Is there *really* a Mr. Anna?' she asked me. "That's Carl's name for my husband Paul," I said.

"One mustn't expect Anna to know she's being kidded unless she's forewarned," Carl said to Emily. I felt my cheeks warm. "And I can only assume that Mr. Anna—who I am quite certain exists—shares her propensity for seriousness."

"Paul's very dedicated to his work," I said, whether in defense of him or myself I couldn't be certain.

"Thank *God*," said Carl in the exaggerated fag-voice I found particularly annoying. "We wouldn't want our nuclear physicists proceeding half-assed. Imagine the consequences."

"They still *do* that up there?" Emily asked, wide-eyed. Could such incredulity be put on?

"It's one of the finest scientific research labs in the world," I told her. "They study an enormous variety of things there."

"Including continued nuclear research," Carl said.

"And how did *you* feel when you heard about the bombs at Hiroshima and Nagasaki?" I asked him. While this was what my father had always retorted to his cocktail party critics, I was shocked to hear his words from my lips.

But Carl merely laughed. "I felt the same as everyone— enormously relieved. Ecstatic, even. It had been a particularly dirty little war, after all."

"If those bombs hadn't been dropped, we might not be standing here now," I said, more of my father's words.

"Perhaps we should call you Leon Junior," Carl said, lightly touching my arm.

I drew away from his touch. "Call me what you like," I snapped. "It's not my business." As I walked away, I heard Carl tell Emily Corbett, "Anna's very sensitive. I must remember not to pick on her so."

"But that was such a long time ago," Emily said. "Too long to still be so sensitive about it." The little twerp. I was only 46, after all.

Unlike my own, my father's stance had never been defensive. My father believed that the Japanese were an enemy who would fight not just to the last man, but to the last person, and that the only way to stop that fight was to either destroy them or to terrify them.

But how does one terrify a people for whom death holds no terror? Japanese tradition views martyrdom, and particularly suicidal martyrdom, as the most honorable death, with death at the hands of an enemy an equally noble end.

Perhaps this might be better explained to our Western sensibilities from another angle: Those who survived the Hiroshima and Nagasaki blasts, called *hibakusha*, were considered outcasts by the rest of Japanese society. Already ostracized by their physical stigmata, they were separated socially as well: They had not died well. In fact, they had done far worse: They had lived.

There is no greater terror for a Japanese than social ostracism, than the dishonor of surviving what should have been an honorable death. Hence the death figures at Hiroshima and Nagasaki were not the numbers that ultimately stopped the Japanese; the casualty figures were.

Did the net result—the end of World War II—justify

nuclear attack? Hindsight has given us photos and statistics that heighten our horror by individualizing it. Hindsight tells us that, because of that horror, an atomic bomb has not been used as a weapon in the fifty years since. Hindsight suggests that the war was close to an end in any event, and hindsight replays Emperor Hirohito saying that, had it not been for the Hiroshima and Nagasaki bombs, the Japanese would not have surrendered.

We of the postwar generation deplore the do-or-die patriotism of our parents, denounce their cheering of Japanese deaths, but we deplore and denounce out of context. How easy for me to be horrified by my father's personal role in those events, to feel tainted, guilty, ashamed. How easy for me to know a cold man, and to decide that his decision to bomb two Japanese cities was cold as well.

Logic, however, does not consider hindsight or horror. Logic tells us that if A = B, and B – C, then A = C. Here is my father's decision, according to that formula: The Japanese will fight until they are stopped. An atomic bomb will stop the Japanese. We will use an atomic bomb.

It does not stop the horrible pictures. But it does help us to understand. And it helps me to see my father in a new light, though I still cannot forgive his coldness.

A volume, or perhaps more than one, of Hana Weissova's diaries was missing, a blank space from 1959 to 1965 that left me once again imagining her life. This time, though, there were new possibilities to insert into my daydreams, and, more specifically, new faces: Carl Mayer's, and my mother's.

Once I knew that my mother and Hana Weissova had

known each other, my imagination knew no bounds. I could picture them sitting behind matched pianos, playing the two parts from Bartok's *Concerto for Two Pianos*, or Brahms's *Sonata in F Minor*. I could seat them on blankets for mountain picnics, strands of dark hair blown about by a light wind, both voices talking at once.

With no real memories to guide me, I had remade Hana Weissova into the physical twin of my mother, and then I'd remade my mother's weaknesses using Hana's strengths. Now I was going further, and creating imaginings that I could wish had actually occurred. There was, after all, no diary to tell me I was wrong.

After favorable reviews of our first performance, the Agua Fria Players were anxious to rehearse a new program, one that might showcase some lesser-known works created for groups like our own. Louis suggested a Villa-Lobos concerto; Paula was anxious to include a work by Josephine Smelker. John diplomatically pointed out that we were a chamber group, not a political organization, which led the other three to burst out all at once, the room quickly filled with the cacophony of their opinions.

"I have a thought," I said into the din. "Excuse me?" One by one, they stopped speaking and looked at me expectantly.

I took the CD out of my purse. *Music of Terezín*, it was called. "Could you put this on?" I asked Emily. She complied, and Gideon Klein's *String Trio* filled the room.

"I know that melody," John said after a few minutes. "My mother sang it to me. She was Czech," he added.

"What is this?" Paula asked quietly.

I stood and retrieved the CD box and passed it around as I spoke. "It's music that was written in a concentration camp during World War II," I said.

"*Written there?*" Louis asked.

"Yes," I answered. We all listened some more. Krasa's *Theme and Variations for String Quartet* began.

"This is amazing," said John.

"*Fucking* amazing," said Emily dreamily. We all laughed, breaking the spell.

"How did you happen to come across this?" Paula asked. I told them briefly about inheriting Hana Weissova's papers and manuscripts, and how my curiosity had led me to the CD.

"Her work has never been performed, so far as I know," I added. "But I inherited the rights along with the transcriptions."

"Are there transcriptions available for these other pieces?" John asked.

"This chamber group found a great many of them, and others they wrote out themselves. If we actually want to do this, one of us should call them. There's a phone number on the CD."

"I'll call," Paula said, surprising us. Paula was not one for social niceties, and made no secret of it. "I'm Jewish," she said. "Thomashevsky. Don't look so surprised. Dykes can be Jews too, you know." We all laughed again, though perhaps a bit more uncomfortably.

"This is so cool," Emily said. "And you don't know why you inherited her stuff?"

"I didn't know initially," I said. "But it seems. . ." I hesitated, then went on in a rush. "It seems she knew my mother."

"Ooh," said Emily. "Karma. Cool."

Something flashed in and out of my memory, so quickly I wasn't sure it really had, and I was less sure of what it might have been. Cool, the flash said. Cool. But there was no image to accompany the word.

August 1958

I shall drive myself mad with this damned symphony.

Although symphonies are usually written in four movements, mine insists on being five. While most begin with an allegro, *center on an* adagio *and then a* minuet, *and end with, well, a* bang, *mine abandons all of these conventions and veers instead in one (or more precisely, many) all its own.*

In addition, it is written for a much smaller group than the usual symphony orchestra: a string quartet, plus a piano, clarinet, and oboe.

It may be presumptuous of me to call this a symphony, but its length precludes any other definition. Perhaps it is operatic in its scope; there is a plot, after all, though there is no libretto to lend it words. The story is told by the music—no, by the instruments—and it is a story that is of necessity fragmented and disjointed, although occasionally two themes intertwine.

It is *presumptuous of me to believe that I am capable of accomplishing this. I am trained, after all, as a pianist, not as a composer (though in fairness to myself I must add that I* did *receive excellent grades in the four sections of composition I was required to study). I have no background in translating a music in my head onto paper without first hearing it played aloud, which is precisely what composition entails. And why a clarinet, and an oboe? Why, for that matter, a string quartet? What do I know of strings, except their particular sound?*

And yet I must do this. Yes, I am compelled. Who else will write this symphony? Who else survived? It is one thing for the historians to say: This happened, and then this happened; for the psychologists to create a new nomenclature for the new psychoses. The journalists write of the horrors and the photographers illustrate the grisly toll, but who hears them? Who will sing this dirge?

Of course, as the dying Hamlet says, "The rest is silence." How to convey such a stunning silence in music? A paradox, that. It is where my lone clarinet comes in, ending, not with a bang but with a diluendo, a slow fade into eternity.

I feel a chill, when I think of this, when I hear that variation's slide into the infinite.

But enough of that. I must say a word about Alice's David, who continues to be precocious in unexpected ways (though perhaps precociousness is inherently unexpected?). He is, first of all, very American. By that I mean he is remarkably self-assured for a child of seven (I should qualify that and say a boy of seven). He is, for example, fearless—unafraid of softballs shooting toward him, of leaping across wide creeks when we hike in the Jemez, of the horrific sonic booms made by the jets at the Air Force base. He does not seem at all nonplussed by the air raid drills schoolchildren are required to perform (they sit cross-legged, hands behind necks, in tidy rows beneath their desks, so that I picture the aftermath—a still-tidy row of little charred bodies). He laughs when I hesitate to cross a street corner because a light is red. ("There's no cars, Aunt Hana. Why should we wait?") He questions his superiors with a markd nonchalance

("I write much better than Mrs. Brown," he says of his teacher). He meets Alice's parental reason with a clever logic that stops her midway through her words. ("Mom. We don't have Nazis here." Of course, he is wrong about this.)

I seek, and never find, signs of my own Pavel within this very different boy. David is already the age that Pavel was when he died, and though he knows Pavel's story well, it is not his story, a distinction he is quick to point out. Physically, David is dark where Pavel had his father's more pale coloring, and psychically, David has a stronger faith— in both himself and in others—than Pavel was ever able to develop.

But because I, at nearly forty, will have no other children, I seek to make my mark on this child in some way. I try to interest him in the piano, or, at the very least, in music, though our only connection there seems to be through country western ballads (he loves to listen to Patsy Cline).

The one place where I do seem to touch David is through my stories. How strange that I should choose a child as the repository for this horror, and yet I find that I have masked them in the genre of fairy tales, a genre that after all houses witches and ogres and wicked stepmothers. The difference is that in fairy tales the children live, and triumph over those who intend them evil; in my stories, the children die.

Here is Pavel's story:

Once upon a time, in a land far away, a land called Czechoslovakia, a little boy named Pavel lived with his Mama and his Papa and his little sister Heidi. Pavel lived in a great stone house on a narrow cobblestoned street, and he was very happy there.

But then, one day, the Evil Men came and said that

Pavel and his family could no longer live in the great stone house. No, the Evil Men said. Pavel and his family must leave everything that was theirs behind and go to live in another town far away, a town that had been built as a fortress, a town that had been named Terezín, but which the Evil Men now called Theresienstadt, which was in their own language, a language that unlike Czech was full of grunts and gutturals.

Why did the Evil Men say they must leave? Well, because Pavel and his family were Jews. How, you may ask, is a Jew different? Pavel and his family asked the same thing, because they *had thought that they* were *no different.*

This was their mistake. A Jew is different in unaccountable ways, in ways a Jew himself cannot see but which others claim to see with great ease. Others will say you can tell a Jew by his shifty little eyes (here David laughs and points out both his and my very large eyes), his huge hooked nose (another laugh, and acknowledgement of our small ones), by his money-grubbing ways, by his duplicitous nature. ("That means two-faced!" David crows, having heard this story before.) A Jew will laugh—yes, like you—and say, "Surely a man who bothers to look will see that those things are not so," but—and here is the thing—these men did not look.

Who can say why they hated the Jews? Why does any man hate another? Often, it is because he thinks the other man has that which he desires. ("That's a commandment," David points out. "Thou shalt not covet thy neighbor's ass." Then he giggles.) Or sometimes it is because he thinks that man covets what is his.

What did the Jew have that the Evil Men desired? Perhaps they wanted Pavel's great stone house. It was a wonderful house, with three stories and many many rooms. Pavel's room was filled with his toys—lead soldiers and elaborate fortresses and houses that Pavel had built from wooden blocks. There was an electric train set from America, which Pavel never tired of rearranging, and there were models of American cars and aeroplanes as well.

You can understand why the Evil Men might want these things.

But what had they that they might think Pavel would desire? This is a more difficult question. They too had great cities built of stone—but Pavel was quite happy with the one in which he lived. They had fat silly wives and fat silly daughters, but, well, Pavel was a little boy. He had a desire for neither.

Perhaps it was their great rivers they imagined worth coveting, but Pavel's lovely city had many rivers of its own, rivers crossed by a variety of beautiful and unusual bridges— yes, they are still there for you to see, should you go.

No, this is not an easy question to answer, why the Evil Men hated the Jews. Perhaps the only answer is that Evil Men hate because they hate. They hate because they are Evil, and Evil does not require a reason.

Good, of course, does not require a reason either. But, unlike Evil, it is its own reward. Evil requires more tangible evidence of its success.

But so. Pavel and his family were sent away from their city to the place called Terezín. Here they no longer lived together, but instead boys with boys, girls with girls, men with men, women with women. Still, little boys adapt. Pavel played with his new friends; he went to the secret school where his grandfather taught. And he drew lovely, lovely pictures, which was a difficult thing, not just because he was a little boy, but because the Evil Men did not allow them to have paper, or crayons.

Yes, these Evil Men were very wicked. But there is far worse wickedness to come.

The Evil Men decided it was not enough to move the Jews from their homes. They decided it was not enough to forbid them to live with their families, or to go to school, or even to have paper or crayons.

The Evil Men decided that the Jews should die.

Now at this time there were many, many Jews. And so the Evil Men had to think long and hard about the best way to kill so many people. First, they tried shooting them at the edges of deep pits which they had the Jews dig. When they were shot, the Jews would fall dead, and sometimes not dead, into these pits, and then the Evil Men would bury them.

This took a long time, and, of course, a lot of pits.

So the Evil Men decided to put the Jews into rooms and then fill the rooms with poisonous gas. This was supposed to be a quick and easy death, but sometimes it was not so quick and easy, and when the Evil Men unlocked the doors they would find the dead Jews piled against them, their fingers scraped raw from trying to escape.

It was possible in this way to kill many more Jews, but the problem still remained of what to do with their dead bodies. For this purpose the Evil Men built enormous crematoria, places in which they could stack the dead Jews and burn them, until all that was left was ash. This ash streamed out from tall smokestacks and covered everything for many miles around, houses and trees and fields and people.

It is not easy to erase the evidence of Evil.

Jews were transported to the rooms of gas in railroad cars. Ostentransportes, these were called: caravans east.

Pavel had always liked trains: remember his electric train set, in his room in the great stone house. So when he was told he would be traveling on one, he was very excited.

But it soon became apparent that this was not the train ride he had imagined. Instead of passenger cars with seats, this train had boxcars, many boxcars, each crowded with far too many people. There were no seats, and there were no stops, except the final stop, at Auschwitz, where Pavel was herded with the others in his boxcar who were still living into one of those rooms, which the Evil Men then filled with poisonous gas.

This story does not have a happily ever after, unless you believe that a hereafter offers that opportunity. But true stories are not often like fairy tales, and for that, I am very sorry.

Georg Frederic Handel is said to have heard the last movements of *The Messiah* in a dream, and the Italian composer Giuseppe Tartini said that his "Devil's Sonata" was first played in a dream by the devil himself. Dreams have similarly been credited as the impetus for paintings including Henri Rousseau's "The Dream" and Salvador Dali's "Persistence of Memory," and for literature including Mary Shelley's *Frankenstein* and Robert Louis Stevenson's *Dr. Jekyll and Mr. Hyde*.

A pre-World War II study explored the dreams of over three hundred Germans between 1933 and 1939. Early in this period, dreamers reported hearing radios blaring propaganda over and over, while, by 1939, a representative dream was that of a man whose recurrent nightmare was that he was being accused of recording his dreams.

But few, if any, people recollect all of their dreams, and even those who do remember some of them recall only small portions. Native peoples believe that dreams are messages from parallel worlds, an interpretation that is strikingly similar to the psychoanalytic belief that they are messages from one's unconscious. Many dream researchers insist that we cannot consider dreaming and waking as two entirely different spheres.

Music, of all the arts, most easily connects these two spheres. By its very nature, it moves us to another state, a feeling of removal from ourselves: Listeners often report feeling "transported" or "moved to tears." This morning I awoke with a lyric I could not place repeating itself in my head, and it was only later in the day, when I sat down at the piano and picked out the tune note by note, that I realized that it was "I've Grown Accustomed to Her Face," from *My Fair Lady*. Melodies haunt us for a reason, as do faces, as do dreams. I *had* grown accustomed to Hana Weissova, though the face I had assigned her was one I had created myself.

It was a dream that drew me back to the cartons in the attic, cartons I now knew had been packed by Carl Mayer shortly after my mother died. In the dream, I was standing on a ladder to an attic—though not my attic and not its ladder—in order to store more things there. My father stood at the base of the ladder, shaking it, and the more I insisted he stop, the harder he shook it.

Then, in the dream, I had a revelation: Rather than continue to store these things in the attic, I could bring them down and keep them somewhere else, somewhere more accessible. I awoke feeling relieved of some tremendous burden, and recollected the dream vividly, except for the fact that I had no idea what the "things" had been.

Still, by mid-morning (it was a Tuesday, a day we did not rehearse), I had resolved to bring the cartons down. I planned to take them to our guest room—hardly ever used as such but nonetheless sporting an always-ready bed and waiting empty dresser. In addition, there was an unused closet, and I thought whatever I didn't keep out of the cartons could be easily stored there.

One by one, I carried the awkward but not-too-heavy cartons down the ladder and set them on the guest room floor. It was close to noon when I finished, and the day had grown unusually warm even for May so I opened the guest room window before making myself a sandwich and opening a Diet Pepsi, both of which I took back to the guest room with me. I sat on the floor next to the cartons while I ate, back against the bed, legs stretched straight out, a posture I'd often assumed as a child but not at all since, and studied the boxes as if their brown sameness alone might reveal something to me. They remained resolutely unforthcoming.

When I finished my sandwich, I began unpacking. I set each item out onto the floor, bed, and dresser without pausing to consider any, and when all was unpacked I stacked the boxes in the closet. I returned to the kitchen only long enough to grab another can of Diet Pepsi and then I sat down crosslegged amongst the cartons' contents to begin my sorting.

My resolve to be efficient—a corner for personal memen-
tos, another for sheet music; a place on the dresser for jewelry, another for photographs—was soon lost to the various
reveries each thing induced. An early 40s score of *Eine Kleine
Nachtmusik* (apparently early 40s as it bore its English name,
"A Little Night Music") brought back a memory of my
mother playing the piece in a loden green sweater set and
pearls. A book of matches inscribed *George and Harriet, May
13, 1957*, called up a child's eye view of pantlegs and skirt
hems, and the sound of mingled adult voices, laughter, and
the clinking of glasses.

I decided to save the photographs for last and put them
into a separate pile without more than cursory glances, as if
I knew it was there that whatever I was seeking lay. When I
had finally finished sorting, I repacked the newly organized
things, labeled the boxes and set them once again in the closet.
I left the photographs out, but it was now too close to sup-
pertime to begin going through them.

I did not return to the room until Paul had gone to bed.
I often stayed up much later than he, so there was nothing
unusual about my doing so this night. I had not, for some
reason, mentioned my day's activities to him, and, because the
guest room was at the far end of the hall and held nothing of
his, it was not likely he would discover my project.

I wondered again about the things I did not tell my husband. Did I think he would ridicule me? That was not very
likely. Perhaps it was that he would attach no importance to
the effort at all, a judgment that would in turn somehow
diminish *me*. My father, after all, had been a master of dis-
missal. "Why waste your time?" was his phrase of choice, an
expression that at once belittled both the effort and the person

making it. We learn quite young what we must keep to ourselves, and lessons learned young are seldom unlearned. Thus I concluded that there was no reason to tell Paul. He wouldn't care anyway, I told myself. I may have even believed me. The chasm I'd imagined lay between us, as if it were truly there.

I turned on the small bedside lamp and spread the photographs across the bed, then propped up the pillows at the headboard and sat down cross-legged against them. The first photos were familiar: my parents' wedding picture; formal portraits of each of my four grandparents, all looking the camera sternly straight-on; my own formal baby pictures, and a series of snapshots documenting my movement from infant to toddler to little girl.

And then there was a snapshot taken with a different camera, a different eye. Standing before the wide doors of a stucco building were my eleven-year-old self, my mother in her black cashmere winter coat, a young and smiling Carl Mayer with a cigarette dangling casually from one side of his mouth, and a dark-haired woman my mother's age.

My breath caught, and I brought the picture closer and examined the woman's features: shoulder-length dark hair worn loose under a stylish hat; large, dark, wide-set eyes; high cheekbones; full dark lips. I studied the hand that clutched a pocketbook, its long tapered fingers, its lack of rings. I noted her clothes: a simple hip-length cloth jacket over a dark straight skirt, low-heeled pumps, the hat that matched the jacket. Was there something foreign about the woman, some lingering pain behind her eyes? I turned the picture over.

And there it was, in my mother's handwriting: *Opening night at Popejoy   Anna, Carl, me, and the pianist Hana Weissova. September, 1959.*

I called Carl Mayer. I didn't care about the time. "I found a picture," I said when he answered. He was apparently still awake.

"Of course you did, darling. I knew there were pictures." Then, "Oh my God—are your repressed memories returning? How exciting!"

"Why didn't you tell me that there were pictures?"

"Why so angry? Is it horrid? Is it graphic, or grisly, or gross?"

I ignored his attempt at humor. "No," I answered. "It's a picture of you, me, my mother, and Hana Weissova in front of Popejoy. 'September 1959,' it says."

"And so now you remember everything," Carl said.

"Everything? No. I still remember nothing. What do you mean by 'everything'? What is it you haven't told me?"

Carl's voice took on a different tone. "Perhaps you should drive down, Anna. Will Mr. Anna mind?"

"He's sleeping. I could leave him a note. But why?"

"Have you read all of Hana's journals?" Carl asked.

"Obsessively," I said, "as you know."

"And even with the journals, you don't remember?"

"Well, there seem to be several volumes missing, from around 1959 to 1965."

"Ah," Carl said, a mystery apparently solved. "Come down. Tell Mr. Anna I've died or something. Come now."

"All right," I said. "I'll be there in about an hour."

Did I know before Carl told me? Had I known and forgotten? I hadn't wondered at the missing diaries; I hadn't wondered why I couldn't remember a woman who'd known me well enough to remember me in her will. I hadn't wondered, until I remembered Carl Mayer, if my mother had known her, though they were contemporaries, and women of similar talents. I hadn't wondered about anything; I'd simply slipped into Hana's life for reasons I'd never really examined.

Carl was waiting at the door when I arrived, and he quickly settled me on his couch and placed a brandy snifter in my hand. "What do you remember?" he asked me.

"Nothing," I told him. "There is nothing there at all."

Carl leaned toward me and put his hand on my shoulder. This is it, I thought. Now I will know what I once knew before. "They were lovers," Carl said.

It wasn't what I had expected. "Oh my God," I said.

Carl kept his hand on my shoulder, and his eyes on my own. "Do you remember?" he asked again.

"No. My God." The snifter shook in my hand and I leaned to set it on the table. Carl sat back.

"Anna," he said quietly.

"Lovers," I said. "My mother. And Hana Weissova. My mother. My mother who was married to my father. Who was my mother."

"Anna—" Carl leaned to touch me again and I pushed his hand away.

"Don't touch me!" I cried. "It's horrible! Why would you tell me such a thing?"

"Because it's true," Carl said. "And it wasn't 'horrible.'"

They were very happy, Anna."

I took several deep breaths, in, out, in, out. "Did I know?" I asked him.

Carl shook his head. "I don't know. You knew they were close, certainly. But your mother took great pains to shield you from their—relationship."

I tried to peer into one of the dark blank spaces of my mind, but saw only a huge wooden door, locked. "I must have found out," I said slowly. "That would explain. Everything."

"Perhaps," said Carl, handing me my brandy again. I took a small sip, and then another. I heard a clock ticking, in another room. I closed my eyes to look again at the huge wooden door.

"My God," I said again, then laughed, a weak, choked sound. "I guess you can give me your therapist's number now."

"Good girl!" Carl said. "Face your demons and cut them down."

"Shakespeare?" I asked.

Carl laughed. "Mayer," he said. "Vintage Mayer. Now you *will* stay the night, won't you? What did you tell Mr. Anna?"

I laughed again and shook my head. "That a sick friend needed me. I didn't tell him it was myself."

And then that night I dreamed.

A long corridor, lined with candlelit wall sconces. I, in a long nightgown, carried a candle myself. A piano played, far off, a Liszt etude, a sound whose distance did not change as I moved down the hall.

And then I was on an elevator, an elevator that turned in different directions, not just up and down but right and left. It was so black, I could not see, and I was alone, except for the Liszt, still far off.

The elevator became a room, a room on the other side of the huge wooden door. A tall bed, and the music all at once close, though there was no piano. Movement on the bed. More darkness.

And then my mother and I were sitting in our kitchen, drinking tea. It was late. "There is something about that particular Liszt," she said, and I said, " 'Tsolidschaya' vodka. Leon's blue suit to dry cleaners. Candles for mother's candlesticks."

My mother laughed. "Clever Anna," she said. "Read between the lines."

"*In dreams begin responsibilities*," I said. "*What evil lurks in the hearts of men?*"

"Clever Anna," said my mother. "Clever, clever Anna. You mustn't ever tell."

Then Hana was there in the kitchen with us, the Hana of the picture, the Hana I had known and not imagined. She sat by my mother, holding her hand. "*Yesterday's ugliness may be tomorrow's beauty*," she said, her voice melodic, pleasingly accented, low-pitched. She was smoking a cigarette that smelled medicinal. *Kool*, said the package.

"Remember, Anna," she said, exhaling smoke with her words. "Do not be afraid." She set down the cigarette and then took my hand and held it. "Remember," Hana said.

Carl was sitting at the edge of the bed when I awoke, holding my hand. "You were dreaming," he said.

"She talked to me," I said. "Hana Weissova. She said, 'Remember. Do not be afraid.'"

"And do you remember?"

I saw again the tall bed, the mysterious movement, but it was in the dream, not real. "I'm too old to return to my childhood," I said, feeling tears fill my eyes.

Carl pulled me into his arms. "There's nothing to be afraid of, Anna. Love is where we find it, not where we seek it."

I sniffled. "More vintage Mayer?" I asked him.

"Vintage indeed. And happily true."

August 1959

I have found a lovely house, one I know I will live in until I die. Set on a tree-lined street that dead-ends at an acequia in the South Valley, it is surrounded by a high adobe wall. The house too is adobe, not at all like my wonderful stone house in Praha, and yet it reminds me of it in a way that is not at all unhappy. It reminds me of the complacency I felt in that house, the peaceful command of my surroundings, the way I could move from room to room and know it was mine, my place in the world.

I was so long without a place in the world. I was without a family, without possessions, and then I rented the little house on Amherst and began slowly to acquire things again. I purchased my Plymouth. I found my Steinway. My dreams began to explore the future instead of relive the past. I allowed myself, once again, to love.

And I am curiously not unhappy. My heart can still ache for Anton, for Pavel and Heidi, for Mama, Papa, and Irena, for all the others, but the heart apparently has a way of healing as well. "There are those who wish to die, and there are those who wish to live," wrote Raja. "Which are you?"

Oh, Raja! I wish to live. And I wish for Anton and Pavel and Heidi, for all of them, to live too, and so I keep them alive in the only way I can, through my music.

Anton was my only sweetheart, the only man I ever loved, and yet my memory of this love is curiously colored, as if there are things I have chosen to forget of it. We used to laugh at him, Raja and I, at his seriousness, at his single-minded pursuit of that which did not seem to matter. The Americans say, "Lighten up," and, had we had this phrase, we would have said it to Anton: Lighten up. Nothing can be that important.

But what was *important, in the end? Was it Anton's belief in economic determinism? Was it my belief in a love of life? Did I live because I loved life, loved it even when it became unbearable? And did Anton die because he did not?*

But then what of the children?

Men are such driven creatures, moving always with a purpose, a plan. Women pause; they reflect; they can juggle many things without dropping a one. Women are capable of loving in a way men are not: They can love without seeking reward or remuneration; they can love because they love.

Anton did not speak of love. "Do you love me?" I would ask, and he would look at me oddly, as if it were a foolish question, of no great import. Yet I knew that he did, or loved the woman he thought me to be, whoever she was.

She is a woman who no longer exists.

A woman can love many people, in many different ways. Those one loves or has loved already are not crowded by new loves; the capacity increases, exponentially.

Such a philosopher I have become!

Back to my house. I move in next month, after the lovely large back room is opened up with windows and a door to what will be a garden. That will be my conservatory. In the garden, I will plant roses and lilacs, spring bulbs of tulips and daffodils, fruit trees and wildflowers, impatiens and mums.

A woman can love many things, many people, and a woman is not afraid to learn from the lessons life offers her. It moves on, life. And so do I. I move on.

How does one begin to rediscover the moments unremembered? I found I could not call Carl's therapist. Instead, I wondered at the intricacies of the piano, read music theory, opened a blank notation pad and scribbled two kinds of notes.

The piano, I wrote, *is unique among instruments for its double stroke. Listeners balked, throughout the ages, at composers from Beethoven to Stravinsky. The ear,* I added, *yearns towards harmony. Reality,* I continued, *is not so simple.*

On the piano, I played a *C. Do,* said the piano. I added a *C* sharp, and the notes complained.

Dissonance assaults the ear, I wrote. *The ear demands consonance, completion. The ear insists that every question be answered, that every incomplete cadence be completed.*

I looked at what I had written and turned to a blank page. Then I put the notebook down and got in my car, drove two-laned highways through the awakening New Mexico summer.

On my way home from these drives, along the Española highway and then up the road that climbs the Pajarito Plateau to Los Alamos, I would try to answer the questions I could not write down. How, for example, do two women who are attracted to each other admit that attraction? How do they consummate it? Does it begin innocently, a hand on a hand, a touch that sends a sudden electricity? I tried to remember that sort of touch, the way I had once felt when Paul touched me, but knew if I remembered, that I would also mourn its loss.

Instead, I tried to remember my mother and Hana Weissova together. I had the photograph, where both faced the same camera. I had the dream, where my mother admonished me not to tell, and Hana insisted I remember. I had Carl Mayer's hand on my shoulder as he said the words, over and over, as if they were recorded on an old stuck 78: *They were lovers, Anna. They were lovers.*

Lovers. Love. Loving. To love: I love, you love, she loves. Love was all I'd ever wanted, all I'd never had.

Evenings, I sat at my piano. I played Hana's symphony all the way through. I practiced my parts for the Terezín concert, set for early July. I played Hana's symphony again, as much as I could on a single keyboard.

The piano could not do that lone clarinet justice.

Nights, I tossed awake in bed, thinking about Hana's notebooks where they lay in the piano bench. Some nights I arose and went to them, seeking hints in what she'd written after 1965, the year my mother had died, hints that she'd loved my mother, hints that she'd mourned her.

There was nothing to find.

The piano duet can take one of two forms: It can be played on one piano (called "piano, four hands") or on two instruments. Unlike a polyphonic arrangement, where one voice sounds the melody and the other the accompaniment, a duet's intention is counterpoint, a dialogue rather than a soliloquy, a harmony rather than a solo.

Composers of piano duets range from Mozart to Ligeti, and the variety of these works reflects this range. The instrument's unique virtuosity is multiplied times two, its capability doubled, its effect twinned.

Not just any two pianists can play a piano duet; just as voices must blend, the pianists' styles must have a certain concordance, a way of being at once individual and paired. The literature of piano technique suggests that this can best be achieved by paying attention to entrances: It is all in the timing, in other words.

As usual, theory here proves far too reductive. While good timing plays its part, as does a particular attention to staying close to the score (another aspect emphasized by the theorists), the successful performance of a piano duet requires far more than mere mastery.

I am referring again to that elusive "heart," but here it acquires a resonance, an echo. Here it acquires both a twin and a mirror; here it acquires a reflective ability of which an individual instrument is incapable. Here is the solo revealed as a chorus, the single voice revealed as every voice.

The duet opens the door.

So perhaps it was like this:

Two women meet, two women of a similar age and appearance, two women who have both learned to shield their hearts. They meet each other's eyes, and it is like looking into a mirror. It frightens them, and they look away, quickly.

But a seed has been planted. Who knows how this happens, the chemistry that is called love? I would like to think it *is* a chemistry, some magnetic attraction of forces much larger than mere mortals, something that makes a particular person's melody play again and again in another's mind.

They meet again. This time, they do not look away when their eyes meet. They have been thinking about each other; they cannot deny this. Perhaps they go out for coffee. They talk, and their voices trip over each other in their hurry to tell all that they must. They laugh, both at once, and the sound is like a sweet harmony, and then their eyes meet again and, across, the table, they each reach a hand, until these hands meet, and hold on.

I tell Carl this story. I tell him in words like these, and he listens, and when I am finished, he smiles and takes *my* hand. "My dear Anna," he says. "You are such a hopeful romantic."

"I believe the phrase is 'hopeless romantic,'" I say.

Carl shakes his head vehemently. "No, no, no. That is all wrong," he says. "Romantics are *hopeful*. They believe, in spite of everything."

I take my hand from his and reach for my tea, a meaningless gesture fraught with meaning. "Is that how it was, though?" I ask him. I don't look at him.

"You would like me to tell you a story, too," Carl says.

"Yes, Carl," I say. "Tell me a story."

I wish I could say I played Cupid, he began. I wish I could say I arranged it, that it was part of some nefarious plan.

But I didn't realize myself it had happened until it already had. All I can give you is what I have myself: the memories of a man who was there.

Do you remember the time I convinced your mother to play with the Opera? Perhaps not. I don't think she brought you with her. It was a dazzling performance. The music is supposed to be secondary to the libretto, but the night that Katherine played the arias meant nothing. The audience stood and cheered for the pianist. Your mother glowed. She glowed, Anna.

But that is not my clearest memory of that evening. This is: After the performance, we went downtown to celebrate. The entire cast was there, and the orchestra, and, of course, Hana Weissova, your mother's dearest friend.

Your mother was constantly surrounded by people. They were congratulating her, urging her to resume her career, or merely trying to bask for a moment in that glow.

I watched her, and when I caught her eye, she looked both pleased and frantic, if it is possible to discern such plurality from one's gaze. But then she looked past me and the fear vanished, replaced by such a sad joy that I turned to see what she was looking at.

She was looking, of course, at Hana Weissova, who sat quietly in a corner, nursing a Scotch. Hana smiled back at her, and that is when I knew.

I made my way over to Hana, and sat down next to her on the little couch. I know you will find this hard to believe, but I didn't know what to say, so I merely smiled at her.

"Look at her," she said, gesturing with her chin, and I did look. Then I looked back at Hana, who smiled and said, "Never believe that you have lost happiness forever, Carl. It will always find you once again. I do not understand, but it is so."

"Thank you, Carl," I whispered.
"*De nada*," he said. "It's nothing."
But it wasn't.

It was mid-July, and hot, but that wasn't why Paul came home from work nearly breathless. "They want me to go to Israel," he said.

"Why?" I asked. I knew who "they" were.

"I can't tell you exactly," he hedged, but then immediately grew excited again. "You can come, too. That's what they said. That I should bring you with me."

I went into the den and sat down, knowing he would follow. I heard him mix our drinks, and then he came and handed me mine before easing into his recliner.

"Why would I want to go to Israel?" I asked. "Take your mother."

Paul threw back his head and laughed, a gesture and sound I hadn't seen or heard for so long that I was startled. "Why would I want to take my *mother*? He asked. "I want to take my *wife*. You know, a *vacation*?"

"But you'll be working."

"So? You can play tourist while I work."

"There are terrorists."

"And there are drive-by shootings in Albuquerque. Come on, Anna. It'll be fun."

Fun? How could this stranger I called my husband talk

to me of fun? But—didn't Raja live in Israel? Hadn't there been something in the will?

"There's someone I might visit there. . ." I began.

Paul flipped his chair forward and came and sat down next to me on the couch. "That's my girl," he said.

I winced; these were my father's words. But I was also pleased that my husband and I were having a conversation that involved us both, and pleased, too, that he seemed excited about something—and that he was sharing that excitement with me.

"And you're a good boy," I said in a voice I hadn't used with him for many, many years. In response, Paul took my glass and set it down, and then he kissed me.

I got her name and address from the lawyer: Raja Ben Tov, 18 Chaim Weizmann, Haifa, Israel.

Dear Ms. Ben Tov, I wrote,
   My husband and I will be visiting Israel in early August, and I would like to arrange, if possible, to meet you, to take you to lunch, to talk to you about your sister Hana Weissova, who I have been told was very close to my mother, Katherine Holtz.
   I look forward to hearing from you, and to meeting you.
Yours very truly,
Anna Holtz Kramer

And then, a mere week later, a letter came back, a lovely pale blue airletter, a lovely pale blue stamp in its corner.

Dear Mrs. Kramer,

I am delighted to her from you! Katherine's daughter! I wondered if I ever would! And you will be in Israel! This is wonderful news! You and your husband will stay with me in Haifa—my house is much too large for one woman who daily grows smaller and her two much-too-indulged little dogs.

You will no doubt want to see the diaries and letters Hana asked me to keep. "Someday Anna will want to understand," she said, and that someday has finally arrived.

Your mother was a beautiful and singular woman, and I am proud to have met her when I visited New Mexico in 1964. Hana loved her very much—but this you already know. Hana's life was not an easy one, and yet she allowed herself joy despite all her sorrow. Your mother was a particularly great joy to her.

As I know you will be to me. I shall count the days until you arrive.

Shalom,

Raja BenTov

I wanted to take the diaries and scores with me but I was afraid they would be lost. My solution was to spend an afternoon at Kinko's in Santa Fe, painstakingly making copies of everything. It ended up costing a lot of money, but the peace of mind was well worth it.

Paul seemed so pleased that I'd decided to accompany him. He'd been to Israel once before, during a high school summer—1967, the year of the Yom Kippur War. Like Raja, he noted Israel's similarity to New Mexico. "But it's different, too," he added. You *feel* the history there. It's in the air."

This was not a way my husband talked, and my desire to know the place increased. And I would meet Raja. *Karma*, Emily would call it. I sometimes caught myself smiling.

We played the Terezín program Fourth of July weekend, and were written up in papers as far away as El Paso and Denver. At the reception following our opening performance, a man about my own age smiled at me across the room. Flirting? I wondered, frightened and flattered. But no—there was a woman with him. And, they were making their way toward me. I tried to match his face to a memory, but was still without a connection when they arrived.

"You don't know me," he began, then stopped when he saw sheer relief flood my face. "Oh, I'm so sorry. Shit." His drink tipped, and the woman—his wife, I was certain now—took it from him with a smile, then extended her free hand to me.

"I'm Julie Stone," she said, "and this stage-struck fool is my husband, David."

David Stone recovered himself, saw that I was trying to place the name. "Hana Weissova was my godmother," he said.

"David Stone! She wrote about you in her diaries. But you were a little boy—"

"And you were a little girl."

I stood still. "We've met."

"It was a long time ago. I've been waiting for you to play a concert, so we could meet again. Your mother meant so much to Hana."

I had a moment's urge to turn and run, and then the urge was gone, as if it had never existed. "And Hana meant so much to my mother," I told him.

"Thank you," he said, and then I was certain it was true.

That night, I dreamed my mother called me on the phone. The phone rang and rang, and when I finally answered, she said, "We cannot blame people when they reach out for love."

"Love is where you find it," I told her. "And if you lose it, it will seek you out, until it finds you once again."

When I awoke, I thought I saw her there, and I reached out my hand toward hers, stretching, stretching. But then my father was there as well, standing between us, and I was confused, because he was dead. *Perhaps I haven't awakened after all*, I thought, and at once I did awaken, truly, this time, shaking and alone. Paul had already left for work.

"Forgiveness," I said aloud. The word was soft and loud in the brightness of the midsummer morning, *pianoforte*, which is also the original name of the instrument that I had chosen to be my voice.

But while I had forgiven my mother, forgiving my father was not so easy. How could he? I would answer myself every time I sought to begin. How could he whistle while he worked? How could he keep my mother's friends from me, myself from me, my life from me? As I'd think these things, my anger would grow and grow, and I began to understand something of the nature of the secret things my husband worked on: the small made large, the mushrooming. *Containment*, I told myself, as if the word were a prayer. But I found that it had lost its power to hold me, and was merely a word after all.

On the long El Al flight from JFK to Lod, neither Paul nor I could sleep. Paul, uncharacteristically talkative, told me stories about his mother's village in Poland, and then, at dawn, moved on to Auschwitz. It must have been our destination that determined this odd choice; he'd never talked of these things before.

"She doesn't understand why she survived," he said. "She says it made no sense then and that it makes no sense now. She saw people come and just as quickly go, day after day. She was the nanny for the Commandant's children, and that's why she was spared. But she doesn't know why it was her. For fifty years, she's tried to understand why it was her, but she doesn't."

"She shouldn't feel guilty," I said. How easy to say that of another, I thought.

Paul turned to me with surprise on his face. "But she doesn't feel guilty, Anna. Many survivors *do* feel guilty, I know. Others feel fortunate, and she's probably felt that, though her memories can't be called fortunate. No. I'm saying it exactly as she does: She just simply does not understand. There is no explanation."

"No," I agreed. "There's not." I wanted to tell him about Hana Weissova then. I wanted to tell him about Hana and my mother, about my father's decision, about my own guilt about his decision, so foolish in the face of a guilt like this.

So foolish, I thought. These women lived through the most horrific time in history, and yet they have managed to go on. What have *I* done?

I turned to Paul. I'd find a way to begin. But now his mouth was slightly open, and his eyes were closed. I let him sleep.

Raja BenTov's sprawling concrete-and-glass house sat high on a hill overlooking Haifa and its bay. Sparsely but elegantly furnished, it was a place that seemed a part of its surroundings, a place that belonged. And Raja BenTov too belonged, as much a part of the place as it was a part of her.

She was small—the same size as my mother-in-law Rose—but like Rose was possessed of an inner energy that belied her 73 years. She wore her bright white hair pulled up into a tidy knot, and her blue eyes sparkled behind bifocals. Her dogs were black cocker spaniels, Moshe and Miriam, and Moshe had only one eye.

"He was born that way," Raja explained as she led me to a screened-in porch at the back of the house, "so his name was a foregone conclusion." She laughed, the laugh of a much younger woman.

A tall black woman—she'd been introduced as a recently arrived Ethiopian Jew—brought a pitcher of iced tea and some little cakes and then soundlessly departed. Below us, Haifa shimmered in the afternoon's heat, not quite real. I had never flown overseas before; this new reality had certain qualities not unlike a dream.

"I am so sorry I could not meet your husband," Raja said.

"Work," I said, with a flip of my hand, a gesture I seemed to have picked up during my five days in this odd country.

I suppose I should have felt out of place: It was full of Jews. I remembered how Eva Marie Saint had looked in the film *Exodus*: taller, blonder, unsure in a way the Jews weren't. But I didn't feel that way at all.

I'd taken a walking tour of Jerusalem after sleeping off our flight, and with each step was reminded of how many had trod these stones before me. I loved the sound of the guide's accent, the words exiting below his huge moustache with a basso whose resonance an American voice could not possibly possess.

Every place had a story, and Yitzhak was a storyteller. My fellow tourists, older American Jewish couples from the suburbs of New York and Johannesburg, often interrupted him, but Yitzhak was patient with them, and could pick up his stories again exactly where he'd stopped.

"Anna?"

I looked up from the shimmering city to find Raja staring at me.

"You were elsewhere," she said, smiling. "It is selfish of me to interrupt, but we have so little time."

"No," I said. "I'm sorry."

Raja stared at me, another Israeli habit to which I'd grown accustomed. "You look so much like your mother," she said.

"I *do*?" I looked nothing like my mother, possessed none of her elegance, none of her inherent grace.

But Raja had risen and now brought a photo album to me, opened it and withdrew an enlarged snapshot of my mother and Hana Weissova. "Come here," Raja said, taking my hand to lead me to a wicker-framed mirror, where she held the photo beside my face. "You see?" she said.

I stared. I did see. While I could know my own image only in a mirror, I had never seen my mother's so. Reversed, she became me. Or I became her. Had this always been so?

I remembered an early evening just before I left for college, when I had sat playing the piano in the fading light. I was playing a Beethoven sonata, the pure notes of the Steinway masking my lack of virtuosity.

I had become aware of my father—standing there, watching me—slowly, and then had not stopped playing until the end of the piece. When I did stop, he did not move for a moment. Then he shook his head, first a quick shake and then a slow left to right that said, emphatically, "no."

I looked at him then, but instead of meeting my eyes, he turned and left the room. I had thought it was my playing, and had covered the keyboard. Now, as I looked in the mirror, I saw that that had not been it at all.

Raja, behind me, reached her hand up onto my shoulder. "You want to see the diaries, too," she said. I nodded at my mother in the mirror. "Come," said Raja. "I will take you to them."

"Thank you," I whispered, my mother still looking back at me while my father retreated to another room.

"*Sha*," Raja said. "*Cum*."

January 1960

Her name is Katherine Holtz and she is the most beautiful woman I have ever met. She is also the saddest, sad in a way I have never been, in spite of everything, sad in a way that has nothing to do with her life but seems rather a part of her in the same way as her shining dark hair, her pale smooth skin, her long and lovely ringless hands.

I love this sadness. How do I explain? Should one not wish to make someone one loves happy? Should one not seek to move them from their melancholy to joy?

But here my answer is no. If we truly love, we love that person as she is, and do not seek to change her. I needed Katherine to teach me this, to show me that this was the way I loved Anton, with all his methodical and practical ways. Anton was not as I am, and I did not wish to make him so: I loved the otherness of him. And I love the otherness of Katherine as well.

How did this happen, that I should love a woman in this way, a woman who has a husband, who has a child, a sad and quiet girl so much like her mother it pains my heart? I did not seek it; I sought no love; I had decided to live my life alone. And surely Katherine did not seek it; she would never leave her husband, for she loves him as well.

Carl Mayer likes to twirl an imaginary moustache and take all the blame: He introduced us, he says, but then I say, That is all you did. You could not know. Though Carl, of course, would like to think otherwise.

The few nights Katherine can stay with me, I cannot sleep. I have learned how precious time is, and I choose to watch her sleep instead. In sleep, I see, she is at peace; in sleep her lips will sometimes smile. "Sleep, sweet Katherine," I want to whisper. "Sleep, and do not cry."

I closed the volume and reached for another, opened it randomly.

September 1964.

I am certain that Katherine is ill, though she has been better during the summer, the dry heat a help, though she does not wish to be helped, or cured.

"Katherine," I will say to her. "You should see a doctor," and she will say, "A man cannot change what the fates have begun."

This is such foolishness I want to put my hands upon her shoulders and shake it from her. I do not, of course, because, no matter how foolish I may think it, I also understand it, understand it in a way that makes me know that this is why I have managed to go on.

A God? No. Some force at work that determines our lives? No. I do not believe that either. Yet there are things over which we have no control, things we cannot change. They are what create our lives, these things, and what we can do is make the best of it, and live those lives, or rail against them, and suffer.

I have seen enough suffering. Like Doris Day, I sing, Que sera sera. Whatever will be will be.

Is this horrible of me? I do not think so.

November 1964.

She sits on the floor by the fire, but still, she shivers. I go to her and wrap her in my arms, tuck the afghan more tightly around her.

"I am not cold," she says, resting her head on my shoulder. She stares into the flames.

"But Katherine," I say. "You shiver so."

"I am not cold," she says again.

"No," I tell her. "You are not cold." I have known cold
people, and Katherine is not one of them.

December 1964.
I have added a last theme to the symphony, a minor
melody which nonetheless has resolution. It is yet another
variation of "Dodi Li," an odd choice, perhaps, since
Katherine is not Jewish. This theme is introduced in the final
movement, and is played by the right hand only, within the
middle octave of the piano. It repeats itself over and over, then
disappears, and is picked up again by that lone clarinet, where
it becomes stronger, purer, and carries on until the end.

I couldn't read on, not yet. I drew the diary's ribbon to the
page where I'd stopped and gently closed it. Then I went and
rejoined Raja on the porch.

"Thank you," I said. I reached across the table to hold
her hand.

"You are all right?" she asked me.

"Yes," I told her. "I'm all right. It's *all* all right. Thank
you."

And Raja smiled at me, a familiar smile, one that I recognized as Hana Weissova's, and that I remembered from
many, many years before.

Of all musical compositions, the symphony is the most ambi-
tious. Lasting as long as forty-five minutes, it is characterized
by four ritualized movements: the dramatic first; the lyrical

second; the dancelike third; and the rousing Finale. While early symphonies were written for small orchestras, it was Beethoven who expanded its scope, and his most famous Fifth Symphony illustrates both his mastery of the form and its elevation to a dramatic scale.

Theorists say that the short-short-short-long motif that opens the first movement symbolizes fate knocking at the door. The second movement calms, but then the third resumes the struggle, leading via a bridge to the Symphony's Finale, in which, some claim, man triumphs over his struggles. This thematic structure became a dominant trend for the composers who followed Beethoven.

Still, by the twentieth century, composers rebelled against the constraints of such strictures. Symphonies were no longer confined to one predominant key, or even to harmonic constructions. Many returned to the smaller orchestra of the symphony's early years; others experimented with new musical forms such as the twelve-tone system and electronic enhancement. The number of movements could be two, or six, or as with Hana's, five.

The questions, though, remain. Does the music reflect the times or do the times create the music? Does dissonance signal chaos or does it cry for resolution? The composers themselves insist that they create what they must, that they find their disparate themes as the music emerges, and that, if there is a Greater Being, it is in music that It will be found.

We all create our requiems the best ways we know how. Most mourn quietly, and privately, while others must commit their sorrow to paper, a medium that in the end is both absorbent and resilient.

On August 6th, Raja, Paul, and I drove to Netanya, on the Mediterranean coast, to the small hillside graveyard where Hana Weissova was buried. It was a Sunday, a work day in Israel, but I'd asked Paul to come, telling him I wanted to visit the grave of a dear friend of my mother's and that I wanted him to come along. The papers that morning were filled with Hiroshima remembrances—it was the fiftieth anniversary of the first atomic bomb—but Israel, a country sadly inured to the realities of war, did not question the decision to drop the bomb the way America had begun to.

We placed our stones on Hana's grave according to Jewish tradition and Raja and Paul said the *Kaddish*. Then, leaving Paul to read gravestones, Raja and I wandered among the graves, mostly recent in this still-young country.

"My father picked Hiroshima," I told her. "I cannot begin to forgive him."

"But Anna," Raja said, stopping to turn and look at me. "There is nothing to forgive."

"All those lives," I said, "And such horrible, horrible deaths."

Raja smiled and shook her head. "Come," she said, gesturing to a bench. "Sit." We sat, angled to face each other. "Do not think me condescending," she began, and I shook my head, "but Americans know nothing of horrible deaths. For you, it is all in the imagination, and the imagination makes it far more horrible than it was, for all that it *was* horrible. Does this make sense to you?" I nodded.

"I saw many terrible things," Raja went on. "My sister Hana, she should rest in peace, saw her own family sent away, one by one, to die. My own husband, Josef, died in my arms, and I left him there, in a Bavarian wood. Your mother-in-law, you have told me, lived under the soot of smokestacks where her fellow Jews' ashes rose from their mass funeral pyres. So your father said, 'Enough.' The Japanese committed atrocities of their own, and your father said, 'Enough.' And I say to you, Anna, 'Enough.' Let him rest in peace. He did what he thought was right."

"You didn't know my father."

"No, I did not. But I knew men *like* him, men who made the difficult decisions they had to make to try to stop the horror. And the horror still goes on, in that bus bombed last week in Tel Aviv, in Bosnia and in Africa, and in places we have never heard of, and still men try to say, 'Enough.' They are only men, Anna. They can only do what they can do."

Paul approached us, then stopped a few feet away. "Whoa," he said. "So serious. Are you all right?"

Raja looked at me, and I smiled at her. "Yes, Paul," she said. "We are all right. And Anna is beginning to understand."

That night, our last in Haifa, Raja handed me a sealed envelope with my name written on it in a fine European script. "It is from Hana," she said. "For if you ever found me, which you have. Go on, open it. I will leave you to read it."

I slit the envelope carefully with a fingernail and unfolded the two thin sheets that lay within.

Dear Anna, it began.

Because your mother was quite adamant that I must never contact you, I must assume that if you hold this letter in your hand you have sought me out yourself, but that I am no longer alive to talk to you. I regret that, but it was Katherine's wish and I would not dream to betray her trust.

There are things that Katherine did not know how to tell you, and so told me instead. Did she wish me to tell you these things? I think, yes and no, but yes and no is also a fitting characterization of your mother, while I was the one who always said yes. And now I am the one who is left, so I will tell.

Your mother loved you very much. You must already know this, and yet, were I certain, I would not feel so strongly that this is where I must begin. She wanted so much for you—love, and good fortune, and happiness—but she did not know how to reach you. She did not know how to reach you because you were so alike, you and Katherine, both so strongly armored behind your carefully built walls.

Late nights in the kitchen, she told me, you and she would sometimes talk. "They were just as late-night kitchen conversations should be," she told me. You did not then seem a child but her treasured friend, someone who could see the dark secrets of her soul and love her in spite of them.

"But she is also her father's daughter," Katherine would say, and then she would shake her head. She loved Leon; she loved him dearly, and yet she saw him for the narrow-minded man he was. She saw this because she too had been narrow-minded when she met him.

"Anna will be all right," I would tell her, though perhaps she could tell from my voice that I was not entirely certain. After she died, I worried about you constantly. I wanted to call you, to see you, but Katherine had said I must not. I pestered poor Carl Mayer incessantly, but Leon had banned him from your life. We to whom your mother was dearest longed to be there for she who was dearest to your mother. But it was not to be.

But your mother was most of all stunned by your talent on the piano. "It leaves me speechless," she said. "I can only grasp the curtain and look out to the canyon while her music takes flight around me." I, too, heard you play, and so I know that this was not merely a mother's pride speaking. Music speaks through you, Anna, and you must not stand in its way. I look for your name in the papers and do not see it, and can only hope that, though you may not be performing, you have not let your talent fall away unused.

Sometimes, when I am in Santa Fe, I imagine that I see you. I imagine that you have grown to resemble your mother, that I will know you at once. If I were to see you on the street, I could not pretend not to know you. "Dear, dear Anna," I would say. And you would answer, "My darling Hana," your voice an echo of your mother's.

I miss her very much.

But most of all I wish you well, Anna. Do not let your past haunt your present or your future. Remember, and forgive. There is time for little else.

With my love,
Hana Weissova

I went to my suitcase and took out the folder with Hana's Symphony. I hadn't shown Raja the score, because, as she'd explained, "I can't read music. It would mean nothing to me."

But hearing it would. I knew there was a pretty little spinet in the living room; perhaps it had belonged to Raja's husband. I carried the music in and moved a lamp so that I could read it, then lifted the spinet's cover and began to play.

Raja and Paul came into the room and stood listening. I played the Symphony all the way through, changing the timbre as best I could to effect the final shift to what should have been a lone clarinet.

In the silence left when the Symphony ended, I heard the sounds of Haifa's night humming through the open windows. Raja moved to where I sat and brushed my hair with her fingers, then left the room. Paul stood by the window, looking out toward the city below us, its lights insisting themselves into the darkness.

"Will you play it again?" he asked. In that moment, I loved him once again, and then my mother and my father, and the woman who had made it so.

"I have so much to tell you," I said.

"I know," he answered, not turning. "But first, please, *again?*"

I lowered my fingers to the keyboard and began, again, to play.

Acknowledgments

The seeds of novels are planted in many ways, and this one owes much to a book I first read in the fourth grade, Gerda Weissman Klein's *All But My Life*. Mrs. Klein's daughter was my friend, Leslie; her book was my introduction to a world far less benign than I had previously imagined. More information on Terezín can be found at the website of the Terezín Chamber Music Foundation: www.terezinmusic.org or by calling the Foundation at 617-730-8998. Their website address is info@terezinmusic.org

Thank you: François Camoin, Lee Ann Chearney, Mark Doty, Judy Fitzpatrick, Barbara Furr, Donna Goldman, Joan Green, Beth Hadas, Anne Hawkins, Phoebe Hemphill, Joanne Sheehy Hoover, Kaitlin Kushner, Sydney Lea, Joanie Luhman, Russell Martin, Kevin McIlvoy, Hope Bussey McKenzie, Dara

McLaughlin, Robyn Mundy, Christopher Nöel, Marianne and Michael O'Shaughnessy, Pamela Painter, Evelyn Schlatter, Donna Smith, Linda Stout, Pari Noskin Taichert, Arlene Tognetti, Judy Villella, Michael and Anita White, and the late great Bette Casteel and Camille Domangue.

Lastly, thanks to my husband, Bob Cook, who has always, and continues to, believe.